ELLY ROBIN
AND THE
COLORADO GOLD CAMP

© 2015 P.D. Quaver

All Rights Reserved Worldwide

Revised Edition: 2019

Volume Two of
The Ordeals of Elly Robin

Elly Robin
and the
Colorado Gold Camp

by P.D. Quaver
with illustrations by the author

Books by P.D. Quaver

Unplugged

The Ordeals of Elly Robin Series:
    Volume 1: *The Ordeals of Elly Robin*
    Volume 2: *Elly Robin and the Colorado Gold Camp*
    Volume 3: *Elly Robin on the Road*
    Volume 4: *Elly Robin in the Big Easy*
    Volume 5: *Elly Robin: Bird in a Gilded Cage*
    Volume 6: *Elly Robin on the Lam*
    Volume 7: *Elly Robin in Harlem*
    Volume 8: *Elly Robin Goes to War*
    Volume 9: *The Triumph of Elly Robin*

Visit P.D. Quaver at pdquaver.com

*To my brothers
with boundless gratitude
and the hope that this evokes
something of our Colorado childhood*

Contents

LIST OF ILLUSTRATIONS / vii

AUTHOR'S NOTE / x

CHAPTER ONE: Cripple Creek / 1

CHAPTER TWO: A Misunderstanding / 20

CHAPTER THREE: The Fourth of July / 37

CHAPTER FOUR: Crapper Jack's / 59

CHAPTER FIVE: An Invitation / 79

CHAPTER SIX: The Man with the Purple Neck / 97

CHAPTER SEVEN: Investigations / 118

CHAPTER EIGHT: Today's the Day / 135

CHAPTER NINE: Surprises / 156

CHAPTER TEN: Escape / 170

AFTERWORD AND HISTORICAL NOTES / 187

SUGGESTED LISTENING / 190

ACKNOWLEDGMENTS / 192

List of Illustrations

"What old Sam means to say is—well, if you does it the
same way every time, you ain't really doin it." / 38

She felt so full of life she could have screamed,
grown feathers and flown, spontaneously combusted. / 46

"She's comin round, Gov'ner!" / 77

By and by they were actually flying through the air! / 104

"You need this money, and I don't." / 111

The plucky little machine bucked and tossed. / 141

Bill and Hannah were locked together in a kiss,
the likes of which Elly had only read—or dreamt—about. / 155

Jimmy lit the rag and a moment later hurled the gas can. / 185

Author's Note

Anyone reading source material from the early decades of twentieth-century America will find the ethnic and racial slurs we now so abhor being tossed around with breathtaking casualness. So the occasional inclusion of these repellent words in the dialogue of my characters stems not from any wish to offend, but a simple desire to recreate the authentic speech of the period—that sense, the holy grail of the historical novelist, of having gone "back in time."

—P.D. Quaver

Chapter One

Cripple Creek

In April of 1911, Elly Robin and Jimmy McGann arrived in the rough steelmill town of Youngstown, Ohio.

It had been two years since Jimmy had discovered Elly's amazing musical ability and talked her into playing in a saloon in a small Tennessee town. She had such a success, the two of them had quickly said goodbye to hoboing forever and embarked on a new life, with Elly as traveling musician and Jimmy fulfilling the role of impresario.

Everything that first time had been so perfect that only later, after playing in a hundred other places, would they realize how lucky they had been. Lucky the piano was a nickelodeon and no piano player's job for Elly to threaten. Lucky the piano had been in good tune (Jimmy would quickly discover how aggravatingly persnickety she could be). Above all, lucky the bartender didn't take one look at the skinny young girl claiming to be a musician and throw them out on their ears.

Then there were the problems that arose whenever Elly finally did secure a playing job. Word would quickly spread, crowds would grow, men would tell their wives about the "little firecracker I heard playing the piano at Abe's last night," the women would talk amongst themselves—and some sanctimonious personage would show up to verify this rumor about a child working in a saloon. Jimmy learned to befriend the bartenders, who would tip him off that the overdressed gentleman in the corner trying hard to blend in was president of the local chamber of commerce or Pastor Erwin's brother-in-law. More than once, they had to escape out the back way and beat it out of town one step ahead of the truant officer or the SPCC—the dreaded "Gerries" of Elly's vaudeville days, returned to haunt her.

"What would happen if they caught her?" Jimmy asked one bar owner.

"Well now, if she ain't got no family, reckon they'd put her in an orphanage."

Elly was amazed. Wasn't getting locked in an orphanage an example of that "cruelty to children" the society was supposed to be fighting?

"Plus, they'd slap a fine on me—and you," he continued, nodding at Jimmy, "you they'd lock up for workin her."

"Workin her, hell!" cried Jimmy, incensed. "I's *protectin* her!"

Which was the truth. For they had found their greatest success in those wide-open, half-lawless towns where "anything went," there were things much worse than a young girl playing piano in a saloon, and they could stay for a few weeks and make a stake. But Elly could never have played in these rough places if she hadn't known Jimmy was there watching over her. She'd seen many fights, and sometimes, in an excess of enthusiasm (she presumed), men pawed at her. But she hated being touched, and Jimmy was always quick to step in.

In such places, Jimmy was often reminded how young Elly truly was.

"But what do they *do*?" she had asked early on, referring to the three gaudily dressed and painted-up women who seemed to be fixtures of the bar in a sawmill town near Birmingham they were working.

"What do they do?" cried Jimmy incredulously. "Why, they's *whores!*"

"I *know* they're whores," said Elly, exasperated. She had certainly heard enough about whores around hobo campfires. But listen as she might, there were certain words describing what the men actually did with these women—words intoned with snickering relish and eliciting knowing leers—that eluded her grasp. "I know that—but what do they *do*?"

At which Jimmy had muttered that she'd figure it out someday, but he was damned if he was going to be the one to tell her.

It was all the more exasperating because Elly was sure Jimmy knew the answer. For he sometimes went out again after escorting her back to their hotel and came back smelling of cheap perfume. And early one morning, she had seen him on the streets of Jacksonville with his arm around a chubby young girl from the saloon. In the harsh light of day her sateen gown appeared tawdry and frayed.

In spite of such mysteries, and their precarious, peripatetic existence, Elly was as happy as she could remember being. Bedrolls on hard, cold ground were things of the past, for they did indeed stay in hotels now (cheap ones—but not *too* cheap, after some unpleasantness regarding bugs). They indulged in plentiful meals at local eateries. And they traveled by train as paying passengers.

Jimmy had at first found paying to ride on trains they could easily have hopped for free to be a colossal waste of money. But in time he had warmed to it, and—embracing a sartorial splendor he would once have mercilessly mocked—his traveling attire now included a suit of gray worsted, matching derby and plaid vest, hand-tooled cowboy boots, and a sealskin coat for cold weather. In addition, he sported a large gold ring with a ruby in the shape of a skull, and a derringer with a mother-of-pearl handle to match the clasp knife Elly had given him. (She'd bought it to replace a knife Jimmy had been forced to pawn so they could eat. It was an article he had treasured—the knife with which he'd killed a Swedish giant threatening to throw Elly from the top of a train; now he claimed it was his new knife that had saved the day, Elly never contradicting him.)

Elly too delighted in spending her new wealth on clothing befitting her success, and within the roomy recesses of her imitation alligator skin satchel were several performing gowns, including a

3

black silk Gibson Girl with lace at the throat and a bustle (an attempt to look grown-up that fooled no one); a quilted robe of vaguely Chinese design and carpet slippers for padding down hotel hallways to her bath; a selection of calfskin gloves; and a tortoise shell brush, comb, and mirror ensemble for fixing her hair, which had finally achieved a respectable length. There was even a side pocket in which Mr. Hoppy, Elly's frog-shaped doll, traveled in splendor.

And, of course, there were books.

These were, after her music, Elly's greatest joy. There was nothing better for a long train journey than a volume of Dickens or Hugo. Professor Carp, her hobo mentor, had kindled in her a hunger for knowledge that, flamelike, seemed to grow the more it was fed. She whiled away afternoons in their hotel rooms reading Nietzsche or Montaigne; in the bigger cities, she visited bookstores and stocked up for their weeks in the cultural wilderness—much to Jimmy's disgust, for it was he who had to lug the enormous leaden satchel up the stairs of their hotels.

"Holy jumpin turnips, Elly! Feels like a whole damn *lib'ary* in here—an a fat lib'arian to boot!"

Jimmy had collected his own trove of belongings in the carpet bag he carried, including a stuffed rattlesnake—coiled, tail frozen mid-rattle, fangs bared—that he delighted in leaving beneath the blankets of their hotel beds to terrorize the maids. And in the bottom of his bag was a compartment full of French postcards, a secret recess that Elly, who had a taste for snooping, had long ago secretly penetrated. And whose contents she had examined with great interest.

But the return of the piano to her life was the chief ingredient of Elly's new happiness, and she played as though to make up for time lost. It was always a part of Jimmy's negotiations with the saloon owners that she be able to practice when the bar was closed. Waking up after a night of performing, she would leave Jimmy asleep, breakfast in a café (bacon, toast, and coffee—she could still not abide eggs in any form), reading while she ate. Then it was off to some bar (still smelling of stale beer and tobacco) to play for herself alone.

She followed her whims. She might search the stack of sheet music atop the piano for new songs, committing them to memory after three or four run-throughs. She would investigate the saloon's piano roll collection, searching especially for ragtime—now at the height of its popularity—and learn the music by playing the rolls and watching the keys go down. And she bought the music to any rags she could find by Scott Joplin or James Scott, delighting in both the names—"Hilarity Rag," "Gladiolus Rag," "Froglegs Rag"—and the way Smiley Hobson, the colored dancer from her days in vaudeville, came highstepping through her mind every time she played them.

She purchased other music as well: waltzes by Chopin and Strauss, Sousa marches, selections from *The Mikado*, "March of the Toreadors," short pieces by Grieg. She ran through the Mozart sonatas she had memorized at Miss Bland's piano or dipped into her collection of Beethoven sonatas, savoring their finger-twisting challenges and stormy physicality.

And she learned to play all of Chopin's "Fantasy-Impromptu," with the parts she had played with her mother and father all combined.

They found a job in a roadhouse on the outskirts of Youngstown and spent a lucrative two weeks there.

Elly was just one month shy of her twelfth birthday. But she had kept this fact a secret from Jimmy (as she still kept so much a secret). He had been astonished to learn that her parents had died in the San Francisco earthquake and managed to pry out of her the terrible admission that she had watched their hotel crumble into dust. But only Mr. Hoppy knew that before the earthquake, Elly had been a child vaudeville star (and there was no chance a mute doll would reveal her secret).

There had been a close call, a man in a bar she overheard telling another, "I heard a little girl once, even younger than this one, playing the hell out of the piano in a vaudeville act. Let's see, what was her name now? Baby something or other..."

But Jimmy took no notice, and the man didn't recognize her. Perhaps this was because she had grown rather tall, her fingers now satisfyingly long, and her beanpole of a body had begun to develop some curves (though she had a long way to go before she could compete with the girls in Jimmy's French postcards). Just last week, strolling through Youngstown's downtown district in search of sheet music, she had caught a man staring at her figure—then watched him turn away in confusion when she looked him full in the face.

She could not decide if this appalled or thrilled her.

Their job at the roadhouse was abruptly curtailed one night when a fight broke out over which song Elly would play next. The two combatants (one plumping for "The Man on the Flying Trapeze," the other on fire to hear "The Skater's Waltz") got so worked up they knocked Elly off her bench, crashed into the open piano, and broke a slew of hammers. With the instrument effectively defanged (not to mention the imminent arrival of the police, for "Skater's Waltz" lay sprawled on his back with a knife in his chest), they made a discreet exit into the back alley.

"They was both drunk," said Jimmy. "Yer shouldn't take it too hard."

That music could arouse such violent emotions Elly found perfectly understandable; it was the sight of all that blood that had gotten to her. Jimmy too appeared rather shaken, and they traveled the short distance to their hotel in silence. But an hour later he lay sprawled on the bed (in the same position as the fight's loser) planning their next move, for once again they found themselves at loose ends.

"Terre Haute," he mused. "Fella was tellin me it's wide-open. Even the courthouse square's nothin but saloons and cat houses—"

Elly was poring over a map and shaking her head. "I want to go *there*."

He frowned at the tiny dot she was pointing to—some insignificant burg on the shore of Lake Erie (whose name he couldn't even read)—and looked at her quizzically. But she avoided his eye. So he finally shrugged, and next day (after a trainride to Sandusky, followed by a short hop on an interurban streetcar) found them trudging north along a rutted road with their heavy bags, not a vehicle in sight.

"So tell me again," muttered Jimmy (as if she'd ever told him in the first place), "what's so all-fired important about this little burg?" But he was long accustomed to Elly's spooky reticence, and wasn't surprised when she only shook her head.

In truth, Elly wished she could open up to Jimmy. But the slim hope their destination would somehow lead her to her mother's family suddenly seemed too far-fetched for words.

What clues she possessed were pitifully sparse. She knew her father had been playing violin on a vaudeville tour and somewhere in Ohio his accompanist had fallen ill. A local girl was enlisted to fill in, they'd fallen in love, and that girl would bcome Elly's mother. But her mother's parents, who were of German extraction, had objected to both the violinist's calling, and his ethnicity (the nature of which Elly, despite puzzling over her surname, was still frustratingly unsure of), and the young lovers were forced to elope.

It caused her mother's family to disown her. Which so traumatized Jane Robin that by the time she died—when Elly was only six years old—she had scarcely ever mentioned her past. So Elly knew neither the name of her mother's home town, nor even her maiden name.

Yet just as Elly had penetrated the secret recesses of Jimmy's satchel, she had explored her mother's trunk, and come upon a box of keepsakes. There she had found a childhood photograph of her mother in Bavarian costume. Another of a couple—the woman handsome but hard-faced, the man with her mother's bland smile and gentle eyes—who were certainly Elly's grandparents. They stood on the sidewalk of what was clearly the mainstreet of a small town. The businesses all had German names—WERTZ SAVINGS AND LOAN, HECKMAN DRY GOODS, BLUMENTHAL'S CAFÉ AND BAKERY; after all these years Elly still remembered them.

And among the rest of the miscellaneous keepsakes (a prize for piano performance, a dinner-dance menu, a letter whose cursive writing six-year-old Elly had been unable to decipher) was something else she had committed to memory. An unaddressed postcard, with a hand-tinted photograph of a crowded pier. And bearing the legend, in white ink: LAKESIDE, OHIO'S SUMMER PLAYGROUND.

~~~

Through budding trees they caught glimpses of a ribbon of water. It was still mid-April and the breeze off the lake was brisk, but they were both perspiring freely (and Jimmy still quietly grousing) when they drew up to a gate. Barring their way was a booth and a wooden barricade, like the entrance to a turnpike. Beyond they could see a row of cottages. Above the entrance a large arch proclaimed, in metal scrollwork:

LAKESIDE

RECREATION—FELLOWSHIP—SPIRITUAL ENRICHMENT

"This it?" asked Jimmy.

Elly nodded.

"Funny-lookin sorta place."

Funny-sounding too, thought Elly.

The booth was empty, so they ducked beneath the barricade. Their puzzlement only grew as they wended their way toward the lake through pretty tree-lined streets and rows of neat, well-kept cottages—here and there punctuated by a tea room or ice cream parlor—and not a soul in sight.

"Why, the place is a durn ghost town!" marveled Jimmy.

At the lake's edge they found a large (and equally deserted) hotel, and beyond it a long, empty pier; with a pang Elly recognized the image from the postcard. The sighing cry of a seagull only added to the scene's desolation. Flanking the pier's entrance were two small buildings with doors labeled MEN and WOMEN—changing rooms for bathing costumes, Elly guessed.

Suddenly the door on the women's side swung open, and a stocky little man emerged. He was lugging a large can of paint and a bucket full of brushes. At the sight of them he froze for an instant—then continued toward them. He was middle-aged, with a round bald head fringed with untamed hair and old-fashioned mutton-chop whiskers. His baggy work clothes were spattered with pink paint, and his smooth face completely expressionless.

"Help you folks?" he said, setting down his load.

Jimmy put on his most winning smile. "Yessir, we's, uh, wonderin where all the folks is at? This place is deader than a funeral parlor."

The little man blinked at him. "Season doesn't open until mid-May."

Jimmy flashed Elly a look of reproach, then turned back with another hopeful smile. "So um, when things start hoppin, is there lots of action?"

"Action?"

"You know, saloons and whores and such."

The little man blinked several more times, his mouth opened and closed without emitting a sound, but his face remained utterly blank; it gave an uncanny impression of a ventriloquist's dummy. "No saloons and whores here," he finally found his voice. "This is a Methodist resort."

Jimmy stared at him. "Methodist resort," he repeated, bemused. "Now there's two words don't sound like they belong in each other's company." He was about to suggest that a saloon on the outskirts of town might make a go of it, when he noticed Elly staring at the man with a curiously intent expression.

"Do you know a family," she began in her halting way.

The man swiveled his head (more dummy-like than ever) and blinked at her.

"They had a daughter named Jane who sang and played the piano...and disappeared when she was eighteen or nineteen years old...perhaps a dozen years ago?"

For Elly, it amounted to a speech. Jimmy gaped at her.

"Last name?" said the man.

Elly shook her head helplessly.

"Can't help you then. Don't pay much attention to all the music-making and hymn-singing and such—my job's just to keep things running smooth. You best come back in June, when the place is full-up. But until then—well, you're both trespassing."

And with these words—spoken as blandly as the rest—he picked up his paints and brushes, and ambled off.

~~~

As they trudged back through the empty streets, Jimmy was tempted to break the eerie silence and ask if it was Elly's mother she had been asking about. But the tears in her eyes had already told him the answer.

Terre Haute turned out to be as wide-open as advertised—ditto Cairo, Illinois—and they arrived at the end of May in Dodge City, Kansas, with their pockets already nicely lined. The town was surrounded by malodorous feedlots full of cattle bound for the meat-packing plants of Chicago, and the town itself full of just-paid-off cowboys eager to be separated from their money. A phalanx of saloons and regiment of whores were happy to oblige them, Jimmy and Elly did their part, and in just a couple more weeks they had more money than they knew what to do with.

They were lying in bed one hot, stinking afternoon in their hotel room, both stripped to their underwear. They'd traveled the South all winter but all spring they'd been heading west. It was as if something were drawing them toward Colorado—and they both knew what it was.

Elly suddenly threw down her book. "It's time," she announced.

"Huh?" said Jimmy. He was practicing double-dealing on the bedspread, without much success.

"It's time to go look for her."

"Look for who?" said Jimmy, still throwing down cards. But his face had colored.

"For Liddie."

Liddie, Jimmy's beloved sister. Who had sent him a postcard when he was locked up in the reformatory, telling him she'd gotten married and moved to Colorado. The last he'd ever heard from her.

Jimmy threw down his cards and lay back, staring at the ceiling. He puffed out his cheeks and let out a long sigh.

"Ya reckon?" he finally said.

They left the next day.

After a hot, dusty train ride across featureless plains, they drank in the cool, clear air of Colorado Springs as though it were an oasis. The bustling young city was dominated by the majestic silhouette of Pike's Peak, and the following morning, they took a narrow gauge train that wound around the mountain's flank toward the gold-mining town of Cripple Creek.

It was the place Liddie and her husband, John Skeets, had gone to join his "pal there with a staik." Elly examined the creased and soiled postcard once more, but that was all the information it contained. That, and the postmark: September 23, 1906.

"Almost five years ago," she remarked, passing it back to Jimmy.

He nodded and returned it to his wallet. The farther west they went, the quieter he had become. In his elegant suit and derby, it suddenly struck Elly how much older he looked. It was almost four years since they'd begun their travels together, and she could scarcely recall the ragged boy with the wild thatch of hair and leather eye patch tied on with a shoelace. Now his hair was neatly trimmed, he sported stylish sideburns, his eye patch was of black silk, and his face had lost its youthful softness. While she wasn't paying attention, Jimmy had become a man.

She gazed out the window. The train was on such a narrow ledge they seemed to be flying through the air—air that had grown thin, for they had not stopped climbing since they left Colorado Springs. The view of the deep gorge below them was both spectacular and terrifying. From time to time they plunged into a tunnel, and the car filled with engine smoke before they exploded again into sunlight. Gusts of wind whipped through the car and threatened to snatch away Elly's hat, a dainty affair topped with black ostrich feathers.

At last, the train leveled out in a high valley surrounded by high hills and distant mountains. On all the hills, the trees suddenly gave out at exactly the same altitude; they looked like the shaven heads of monks. Snow still unmelted in June filled seams in the rock, creasing the hilltops like livid scars, and mine shafts punctured their sides like bullet holes. Tents littered the lower slopes like confetti, other flimsy structures flashed by, then the backs of buildings—

And they arrived in Cripple Creek.

With uncharacteristic lack of economy, Jimmy suggested they put up at the National—by all accounts the best hotel in town—and Elly understood it was so he could impress Liddie. But she had no chance to enjoy their splendid room, or even to bathe and wash the cinders from her hair, for Jimmy was in a fever to find his sister.

Their search was a dispiriting affair.

Even if half its buildings looked thrown up in a day, Cripple Creek turned out to be a big place. Jimmy asked one filthy, bearded miner on the street exactly how big, and he grinned and replied that Cripple was a "seventy-five salooner." There were indeed many long blocks of them. As Jimmy went from table to table in each one asking if anyone knew John or Liddie Skeets (and getting no takers), Elly couldn't help but notice the many places with pianos doing good business.

The sun set, and it was instantly so cold they had to go back to their hotel for their coats. They ate a hasty, silent meal and resumed the search. Elly had a headache and seemed unable to catch her breath; Jimmy said it was because of the altitude. On and on they trudged, growing ever more light-headed and discouraged.

At the last saloon on the street, a dark-skinned colored man was playing the piano. While Jimmy made the rounds with his question, Elly stood and listened. The man was nattily dressed in a checked suit, and his left hand was driving the rhythm of the song "Red Wing" in a wonderful way.

Again Jimmy had no luck. He bought some whiskey and a Coca-Cola for Elly, and they sat at a table.

"How two people could live somewheres almost five blessed years, and don't nobody know them… It ain't natural," he muttered, then proceeded to silently and steadily drink.

Elly had never stopped listening to the piano player, who had a way of ornamenting a melody that fascinated her. He was playing a catchy tune she'd never heard, singing the lyric in a pleasing, penetrating tenor:

Come on and hear, come on and hear,
Alexander's Ragtime Band.
Come on and hear, come on and hear,
It's the best band in the land…

The song was such a success he had to repeat it twice. By that time she had learned it, and Jimmy was drunk. So drunk that when they left, he couldn't remember where their hotel was, and Elly had to lead him back and put him to bed.

In the morning, she left Jimmy snoring and went out to pursue an idea of her own.

During yesterday's search, she had noticed many houses with signs like "Rooms for Rent" and "Room and Board, reasonable" posted on their front windows. Steeling herself, she approached the first one she came to and knocked on the door. A harassed-looking woman in a cap and stained apron, wielding a huge ladle like a weapon, answered the door.

"Yes?"

Elly tried to look her in the eye but could only focus on a greasy gray lock of hair escaping from her cap.

"Did you, did you ever have John Skeets staying here? And his wife Liddie?"

"Don't know em," said the woman, starting to close the door.

"Five years ago?"

"Said I don't know em," snapped the woman. She slammed the door.

Over and over the same response. She was beginning to worry that Jimmy might be awake and wondering about her, and was just heading back when she passed a forlorn looking establishment with the sign MOFFET'S BOARDING HOUSE posted on the unpainted front door. A little girl in a dirty pinafore was squatting in front of the house in the dust, trying to mend the shattered face of a porcelain doll with an amalgamation of sand and spit. Absorbed in her impossible task, she took no notice of Elly as she climbed the steps and knocked on the door.

Yet another harassed-looking woman in an apron, taller and younger than any of the others, answered the door, releasing the fragrant aroma of something baking.

"Can I help you?"

"Do you know John—"

"Moosie!" cried the woman, rushing down the steps past Elly. "Your nice clean pinafore, oh Lord..."

She snatched up the child, brushed at her pinafore, put the broken doll in her chubby hands, and carried her back up the steps.

"I'm sorry," she said. "She's an imp. If I don't watch her every second..." She made a face at the little girl, who pouted back at her. "So, you were saying?"

Elly made her little speech. At the mention of Liddie, something changed in the woman's face. "Liddie," she repeated.

"They came here almost five years ago," said Elly. She held her breath.

"Yes, they surely did. And stayed here more than two of those years. John and Liddie. Well of course I remember them. Why?"

"Because she's my sister," said Jimmy, standing at the door half an hour later.

"Your sister," said the woman. She was taller than Jimmy, a big-boned, big-handed woman with a long horsey face but pretty gray eyes. She regarded Jimmy thoughtfully. Moosie peeped at them from behind her skirts. "Yes, I can see it," she murmured to herself. "Well hey, I guess you better come in then."

They followed her inside to a threadbare but neat little parlor full of mismatched furniture. The house was still filled with the aroma of what Elly had decided were baking pies. She and Jimmy sat together on a horsehair sofa while the woman sat in an armchair facing them. Moosie pitched herself across her mother's lap and lay sideways, with her thumb in her mouth, gazing at them.

"It's Jimmy, isn't it?" said the woman suddenly. Jimmy nodded, pleased. "Yes, she talked about you. I'm Hannah, Hannah Moffet. This here is Moosie." She ruffled the child's curly hair affectionately and looked enquiringly at Elly, who murmured her own name. There was a silence. "So," said Hannah finally. "I take it you're trying to find her?"

"Yes ma'am." Jimmy leaned forward, his derby in his hands. "If you could just tell me where—"

"Oh Lord," said Hannah, "I wish I could. But I've not seen poor Liddie since—well, going on more than two years now, and then just passing on the street. I'm afraid I've no idea what's become of her." She was still nervously stroking her daughter's curly head.

"Why 'poor'?" said Jimmy.

"Pardon?"

"Why did you call her 'poor Liddie'?"

"Oh Lord." Hannah shut her eyes, bit her lip, then looked at Jimmy again. "You don't know anything, do you? About what happened to them?"

Jimmy went pale. He shook his head.

Hannah shut her eyes again. Her face seemed to grow red with the effort of holding something in. "Oh that poor child!" she finally exploded. "What was she when she came here—all of fourteen?"

Jimmy nodded. "Thereabouts," he murmured.

"Fourteen. And him not much older. And her already eight months gone. Just kids. Not that I was a whole lot older, but they made me feel like—" She stopped suddenly, her eyes on Jimmy. "You didn't know, did you? About the baby?"

He shook his head dumbly. She bit her lip again. "So, me and my big mouth were saying—oh, but I've got to tell it all, don't I, you'll need to know..." She bowed her head, still absently stroking Moosie. The little girl continued to stare at them. Her eyes were of the same pretty shape as her mother's, but of a startling bright green. Finally Hannah lifted her head and looked at the ceiling. "Lord," she enquired of it, "Lord, do I have to?" She must have heard an answer, for she nodded sadly and gazed at Jimmy again, her eyes gone soft.

"Well, she had that baby, had it right here in this house. Little boy. Sam, they called him. Blonde, like a little angel. Face like Liddie's, and you know what a pretty thing she was. Which was maybe part of why things—Oh Lord!" she suddenly scolded herself. "Who am I to say? Things just happen sometimes, terrible things, no rhyme nor reason..."

Her voice trailed off. Moosie was staring up at her, thumb in mouth. Hannah stroked her face. "This one here, she was six months older than Sam. When he got a bit bigger, they would play together, which mostly was her beating up on him, cause she was bigger. Didn't ya, huh?" she chided Moosie, pinching her cheek.

Jimmy watched them, still as a statue.

Hannah appeared to collect herself. She took a deep breath.

"All right. What happened was, when Liddie got her looks back—and it didn't take long. Not like me, I never got em back cause I never had em to begin with!" She barked a laugh. "Anyway, men looked at her. She didn't encourage them, but she didn't discourage them neither. Truth be told, I think she didn't notice. Cause she loved that little boy to death—" She bit her lip. "The two of them off in their own world, no room for anyone else... Anyway, like I said, men noticed her. Couldn't help but. And John—did you know him?"

Jimmy shook his head.

"John turned out to be one of those boys—can't call him a man, wasn't any older than you—one of those crazy, jealous individuals. I mean worst case I ever saw. Any man Liddie even *looked* at—and they're living in a boarding house full of em!—well, we'd hear him going at her that night through the walls, calling her just every kind of name. No, he never hit her," she said, noticing Jimmy's expression. "I wouldn't have stood for it. His friend Lucas, the one who brought them out here—did you know him?"

Again Jimmy shook his head.

"Well, Lucas was a peculiar sort of boy, not much for words. But he tried to talk sense into John. We all tried. But it was a kind of madness possessed that boy. For then he got it into his head that, well—" Hannah bit her lip. "Got it into his head that Sam wasn't his. Nonsense, of course," she added, staring hard at Jimmy. "We'd hear him screaming at her at night, trying to get her to admit it. Next day she'd cry on my shoulder. Said she thought she was going crazy too."

She hung her head for a moment. Then continued on in a low voice, hardly pausing for breath.

"One day Sam disappeared. It was after he was walking, so at first we thought he'd just wandered off. But we couldn't find him anywhere. Other people joined the search. Someone ran off to the mine to get John and came back with the news that he never showed up for his shift. Well by now, there were more than twenty people searching all around here, and they found Sam. At the bottom of an old mine pit. With a broken neck and his face all battered. And John—well, it seems John had left town on the morning train with all his gear."

Jimmy was squeezing the rim of his derby so hard his knuckles were white.

"What about Liddie?" he said.

"What about Liddie?" repeated Hannah in a voice suddenly gone hard. "What about this poor young girl Mr. John Skeets left behind with a murdered child, a broken heart, and not a penny to her name?"

Moosie, whose curly hair her mother had been nervously twisting during this speech, began to cry. Hannah picked her up and shushed her, then continued: "Left her with nothing. Not that he had anything to leave, him just another poor contract miner like all the rest, for his friend Lucas's claim never panned out. You'll find that's the way of it here—for every one making real money, there's five hundred just scraping by. And Liddie, well, I offered to keep her on, doing housework and such, but a few days later she was gone. No goodbye. I saw her on the street a couple of times—" Hannah opened her mouth to say more, then seemed to think better of it. Finally she continued: "Well, I waved at her, but she looked the other way. But I've not seen her now for a couple of years at least..."

Her voice trailed off. Moosie fidgeted in her arms, and she put the child down. She watched with a wry expression as her daughter snatched up her broken doll and skipped away, then faced them again.

"But you know," she said, "I know lots of people here. I could ask around for you. There's probably someone knows what's become of her."

Jimmy sat so rigidly he might have been carved from stone. Hannah looked helplessly from him to Elly, who found herself strangely unafraid of the big, ungainly woman's kind gray eyes. Looking straight into them, she shocked herself even further by speaking words she hadn't even planned.

"Can we stay here?"

Hannah raised her eyebrows.

"With you?" added Elly. "While you're asking about Liddie." With this her courage was exhausted, and her eyes settled on Hannah's big feet. She felt Jimmy stir and knew he was looking at her and felt herself blush.

"Well," said Hannah, "I suppose I might find room for you. It's not fancy, but I keep my men well fed." She looked enquiringly at Jimmy.

He tore his astonished eye from Elly, looked at Hannah, and nodded.

Chapter Two

A Misunderstanding

They moved their things from the hotel that afternoon.

"I'm putting you in with Zachary Crabbe," Hannah told Jimmy. "He's not much older than you, and I'm told he doesn't snore much. But Elly, well that might be a problem." She stood, chin in hand, and thought. "Well, there's a closet under the stairway," she mused. "If we emptied it out, might be just big enough for a bed…"

Jimmy looked stricken. "Ma'am," he said, "we's always been—I mean to say, we always rooms together. Elly an me."

Hannah stared at him.

"I mean to say," said Jimmy, twisting his derby in his hand, "I always say she's my sister, like."

"But surely she's—isn't Liddie your only sister?"

"Um, uh-huh, she is. But Elly's—I guess the way of it is, Elly's like—well, she's my *pal*."

Jimmy had gone scarlet. Hannah looked from one of them to the other in amazement.

"Well not in my boarding house you don't," she said finally.

And that was that.

In truth, Elly was rather relieved, for there had been a recent occasion when Jimmy had drunkenly begun to caress her in the middle of the night (she had indignantly kicked him away, and the next morning he wouldn't look at her). Besides, the tiny space appealed to her. She helped Hannah clear out stacks of old bedding, an empty birdcage, and a bucket with a crank on top that Hannah told her was for making ice cream. They put most of it on the back porch, where they found an old metal bed frame with a thin, lumpy mattress. Hannah proceeded to beat the mattress—dislodging a pair of disgruntled mice—and they dragged the whole affair inside, almost filling the tiny room. A cracked mirror they'd found while cleaning out the closet was hung on the wall, and Hannah came up with an old kerosene lamp. Together they dragged an ancient camel-back trunk to the foot of the bed to serve as a clothes chest, and Hannah helped Elly unpack.

"Such a lot of pretty dresses," she observed. She held up a yellow sateen gown with ruffled trim and eyed it speculatively.

"For working," said Elly.

She didn't notice the strange look Hannah gave her.

They were just getting the last of Elly's things put away when there was a thunderous clumping sound overhead.

"Guess you'll have to get used to that," said Hannah blithely. "Miners are back from work—and I've got to see about our supper. Bell's at six."

She squeezed Elly's shoulder and rushed off.

The promised clang of a bell came a short time later, and Elly made her way to the cramped, windowless dining room. Light came from a single kerosene lamp suspended above a large round table covered with an oil cloth. A chubby girl, not much older than Elly, was carrying platters of food from the kitchen and slinging them on the table with a put-upon air as the miners filed in and took their places. They had washed their faces and hands. But except where their goggles protected them, the grime had sunk deep in their pores, and the pale skin around their eyes made them look like raccoons.

Hannah entered carrying a big iron pot. The miners passed up their bowls, and she proceeded to ladle out stew.

"Now you men," she said, "now that we have a lady present"—she nodded toward Elly—"I expect you to watch your language."

"Well what about me?" said the servant girl in a saucy voice as she went around the table pouring coffee.

"Martha"—an old bearded gnome of a man with twinkling eyes grabbed the girl around her thick waist—"you ain't no lady."

"Hell I ain't!" said Martha, slapping his hand away and spilling coffee on the floor.

"Lord, give me strength," murmured Hannah, glancing toward the ceiling. She said a short grace, then all talk ceased as the men fell upon the food. There was homemade bread and butter, the stew was thick and rich, and not until the last pieces of bread sopped up the last drabs of gravy did conversation bloom anew.

"Good, Hannah," said the man sitting next to her. He had receding blonde hair, a strong-jawed face adorned with a red mustache, and striking pale blue eyes that fascinated Elly.

"Thank you, Bill," said Hannah, looking pleased.

"Ol Turnip Tom says he's makin a go of the Princess Alice," said a thin miner with drooping mustaches and almost no chin.

"Aw, that vein's played out," said another.

"I heard he's getting four ounces a ton," said a third, in a Scandinavian accent that made "ton" sound like "tone."

"He's spreadin that lie cause he's lookin to sell. I know it for a fact…"

The debate on the Princess Anne (which Elly had concluded must be a mine) and Turnip Tom's rectitude—or lack thereof—was quashed by the arrival of three apple pies, which Martha slung on the table with the same lack of ceremony. They were as good as they had smelled and quickly dispatched. A couple of the miners excused themselves, but the rest pushed back their chairs, rolled cigarettes or inserted plugs of tobacco into their cheeks, poured themselves more coffee, and seemed to settle in for a good talk.

All through the meal, glances had been flashed at Jimmy and Elly, and even as the conversation—mostly about mining and difficult to follow—swirled around them, they found themselves being eyed with open curiosity. At last, the man with the striking blue eyes introduced himself to Jimmy as Bill Wynn and asked him if he was looking for work. The table fell silent to hear his answer.

"No sir. I's lookin for my sister."

"Liddie Skeets," said Hannah. "Pinky, you remember Liddie?"

The gnomish man's eyes lost their twinkle, and he nodded soberly. "Couldn't never forget that poor girl."

A couple of others showed by their looks that they'd heard the story.

"Any of you men heard what became of her?"

Nobody answered. But Elly thought she detected some uncomfortable looks.

"What about that pal of theirs, that boy Lucas?" said Pinky. "He still around? He mighta heard somethin."

"You know, I've no idea," said Hannah. "He moved out right after—well, after all that business. Such a peculiar boy he was…"

"Wait—did you say 'peculiar'?" asked a very young man with slicked-back hair, sparse beard, and gold-rimmed spectacles. "You must be talking about Lucas Cornwall. Works at Smithson's machine shop. Dab hand with a wrench, they say."

"Cornwall!" said Hannah. "Yes, that was it—"

"'e's a dab hand, all roit," said another man with spectacularly crooked teeth and what Elly was sure was an English accent. "If you can get 'is attention."

"So where can I find this Smithson place?" asked Jimmy.

Zachary Crabbe, Jimmy's roommate who reputedly "didn't snore much," was dragooned by Hannah into taking them next day to the machine shop on his way to the mines.

It meant they had to wake up earlier than they ever did and breakfast with the miners. Waking up turned out to be no problem for Elly, because the miners' boots thundering on her ceiling next morning were louder than any alarm clock. As if that wasn't bad enough, she had discovered that the thin wall behind her bed adjoined the kitchen, and the clanging pots and pans sounded as though they were under the bedclothes with her. She hurriedly dressed and dragged herself to the dining room, where she found Jimmy looking just as haggard.

"That what she said bout him not snorin, that was a damned lie," he groused to her.

In comparison with dinner, breakfast was a hurried, silent affair, and soon they set off behind the offending Crabbe, a silent, pimply youth with a lock of hair covering his eyes and a furtive manner. Though it was almost July, the streets glistened with frost. All around them trudged men carrying picks, shovels, coils of rope, lunch pails. At the edge of town, Crabbe pointed to a large wooden building with SMITHSON painted on the side in fading gray letters and left them without having uttered a single word.

Inside the building it was cold and dark. The smell of oil and rust evoked powerful memories in Elly of her life as a hobo, and as her eyes grew accustomed to the gloom, she realized they were surrounded by disassembled machinery. In the corner, where a coal stove gave off a faint heat, the glow of a lantern revealed the crouching figure of a boy. He was perhaps in his late teens, with an unruly thatch of bone-white hair and skin so pale that he seemed all of a piece, as though carved from a block of ivory. He was bent intently over a machine whose case was split in half so that its mechanical guts were on display. Precisely-shaped bits of metal littered the floor. They watched as he slid a piston down the length of a smooth, oiled chamber until it stopped, measured something with a pair of calipers, made some arcane adjustment with a precise-looking tool—then repeated the process of moving, measuring, and adjusting, taking no notice of them.

Jimmy cleared his throat. "Um, hey, scuse me," he said.

The boy continued working as though deaf.

"Hey, so, your name Lucas? Lucas Cornwall?"

The subtlest of nods.

"Okay, so, well hey, I'm lookin for Liddie Skeets."

At that the boy finally ceased his motions, though he still did not look up.

"On account a she's my sister."

Lucas cocked his head like a dog hearing something in the distance. His pale blue eyes had a far-away look.

"So, well, uh, yer know where she went?"

Lucas shook his head and started in working again.

Jimmy made a disgusted sound. "Well now, it sure looks like you jus don't care nothin about her."

At that Lucas paused and finally looked up, though his eyes remained strangely unfocused. "I care about her," he said in a soft, flat voice. "I don't know where she is." And he turned back to his work.

All through this—even though she was almost as intent on finding Liddie as Jimmy, if only for his sake—Elly found herself transfixed by the machine laid bare before her. How often she had stared at broken-down engines in train yards, trying to work out how the parts functioned! But only now—watching the piston slide up and down the severed cylinder, valves opening and closing at each end with fluid, synchronized motions—did she see, with a sudden flash of insight, how expanding steam could be elegantly converted into power.

"Elly, come on," said Jimmy impatiently.

Still she stared. "What is it?" she finally asked.

"Steam drill," murmured Lucas without looking up.

"It's beautiful."

Lucas stopped again and raised his unfocused eyes in Elly's direction. A ghost of a mile appeared on his pale face. He nodded.

Jimmy stood with his hands in his pockets, watching both of them with a disgusted look. Elly finally turned to follow him, looking back over her shoulder.

"Can I come back and watch you?" she said.

Lucas was back at work. But she saw him nod.

Outside the sun was full up, the day rapidly warming. The sky was the bluest Elly had ever seen. As they walked back toward town, she could feel Jimmy staring at her with a quizzical expression.

"That feller," he finally blurted. "Holy jumpin turnips, Elly—that feller was just like you!"

~~~

An hour later, Elly lay on her bed propped up on pillows, the door cracked open for light, trying to read. But Jimmy's words continued to echo through her head. Finally she decided it was hopeless, threw her book down, and stared at the ceiling.

She had long been aware she was somehow different from other people. But to herself, of course, the abilities that astonished others seemed perfectly normal. And the things she couldn't do, things most people found so easy—to look people in the eye, to laugh, to chatter about nothing—these things she had never wasted time worrying about. Until now, that is. For Jimmy's observation forced her to confront what she seldom considered: how she looked to the world.

Again she ran through her memories of that morning's encounter with the boy named Lucas, the boy Hannah and the others had called "peculiar." His concentration on his work, to the exclusion of everything else. His abrupt, terse way of talking—no words at all if a nod of the head would suffice. His toneless voice and unfocused gaze.

Substitute a piano for the steam drill, and Jimmy was right: it might as well be a description of herself.

Elly was appalled. She knew she would soon become a woman and already had vague romantic yearnings. And took for granted that—like the women in the novels she read—she would have suitors, men fascinated by her, men under her spell. But what kind of spell could one so peculiar every hope to cast over anyone?

She was diverted from these dire thoughts by a shadow that fell upon the quilt—and looked up to see the face of a curly-haired moppet framed in the doorway.

"Whatchoo readin?"

For a moment Elly was startled; she had almost decided Moosie was mute.

"A book," she said.

"Is it the Bible?" asked Moosie. She grabbed the door handles and began to swing on the door.

"No," said Elly—and hated herself for her one-word response. Moosie seemed to have lost interest in any book that wasn't the Bible and swung back and forth with athletic abandon.

There was a crash from the kitchen, and they heard Martha utter a word Elly often heard in saloons.

"Can hear…good in here," observed Moosie, panting.

Elly racked her brains, determined to keep the conversation going. She picked up her book. "It has pictures," she said.

"Pitchers?" The room was so small Moosie was able to swing from door to bed without the inconvenience of having to touch the floor.

The book was *The Hound of the Baskervilles*, evidence of Elly's current fascination with Sherlock Holmes and the art of detection. She leafed through the pen-and-ink illustrations one by one. Moosie examined them all, lingering on the picture of the eponymous hound, which she studied gravely. Gratified by this display of reverence, Elly picked up Mr. Hoppy from his nest amongst the pillows and introduced him.

"Mr. Hoppy," repeated Moosie. She proceeded to make the rather battered frog hop about the bed, adding enthusiastic sound effects.

"Martha," they heard Hannah's voice from the kitchen, "I'm going to market. Maybe you might want to peel those potatoes."

The wall was so thin, they could hear Martha sigh.

"That's just a polite way of *tellin* me to peel them."

"You know what? You're right!"

They heard Hannah's bark of a laugh. A moment later she was calling for Moosie, who dropped Mr. Hoppy, jumped from the bed, and burst from the room.

"Moosie!" exclaimed Hannah. "That room isn't your—oh, Elly! I didn't know you'd returned. Did you find Lucas?"

Elly nodded, then forced herself to speak. "He didn't know where Liddie went."

"Well, it was rather a long shot, especially considering how peculiar the boy is. But hey, I'm going marketing. If you want to tag along, we might run into someone who knows something."

~~~

The market was right next to the train station because, as Hannah explained, everything they ate—save for fish people caught in nearby streams and the odd deer shot in the surrounding hills—had to come by rail. It made for prices two to ten times those of any normal city; she'd seen eggs as high as fifty cents each, flour at thirty dollars a barrel.

"Sometimes it's all I can do to charge reasonable rates and still keep my miners well fed."

Moosie stopped in the middle of the street to stare at a squashed and dried-up rat, and Hannah gave her arm a yank.

"But I have my pride," she continued. "And I refuse to skimp. Everyone says my pies and cakes beat all. But Lord, some months I hardly break even, and Bill—Bill Wynn, you met him last night—he says my pride's going to do me in. Not to mention this one here." She lifted Moosie's chubby hand accusingly. "Just last month she got into a whole case of canned peaches. Beat each one open with a rock and drank all the juice. We had peach pie five days straight."

This font of information was punctuated by the purchases of a smoked ham, four cabbages, and a five pound bag of coffee from the vendors next to the station, all accompanied by good-natured haggling and the question of whatever happened to Liddie Skeets. But, other than the general agreement she'd left town, nobody seemed to know.

Hannah added the coffee to her overflowing basket and, as they headed back, opened a new subject.

"So, Elly, all those dresses of yours—you said they're for working?"

Elly nodded, then—still brooding on her inability to chat—forced herself to say "Yes." It was a talent enjoyed by people in books, people in real life—everyone in the entire world, it seemed, except her and Lucas. What made it so difficult? Was it somehow connected with her freakish abilities?

Concentrated on these thoughts, she was fatally inattentive to the direction their actual conversation was taking.

"So," Hannah was saying, "where is it you work that would require dresses like those?"

"Saloons," said Elly.

"Saloons," repeated Hannah.

There the conversation languished, Elly dismally noting her inability to spin it out to a respectable length—and hardly registering how quiet Hannah had suddenly become.

The boots thundered above Elly's head again late in the afternoon, awakening her from a nap. The miners were back, and it would soon be dinner time. And then what? How strange it was not to be working. After a week away from the piano, she was itching to play. She wondered if she should look for a playing job in Cripple Creek while they were searching for Liddie?

She was brushing her hair when she heard Hannah through the wall say, "Hey, Bill."

"Hannah."

Elly had worked out that the kitchen table was directly on the other side of her wall; she heard a chair scrape as Bill sat down next to Hannah.

"Martha," said Hannah, "would this maybe be a good time to set the table?"

"No, it's not a good time," groused Martha. "It's too early. But you're just being all polite again and really—"

"Really I'm *telling* you, you betcha," agreed Hannah.

There was a clang of jangling metal as Martha gathered her forces, then the silverware seemed to march away. Elly smiled to herself and resumed brushing her hair.

"Oh Bill, you know that new girl, Elly?" said Hannah in a low voice. Elly left off brushing again, straining to hear. Bill murmured something. Hannah began talking about Elly's gowns, then burst out with: "Oh Lord, Bill, I'm so afraid that boy is… well, he's taking her to saloons, and—oh Lord, I can't say it."

There was a silence.

"But Hannah," said Bill finally, "do you *know* this?"

"Well what else would she be doing in saloons wearing dresses like that?"

Elly felt the blood rush to her face.

"But how do you know that—"

"That she works in saloons? Oh Lord, Bill—the child TOLD me, just as bold as you please!"

There was another long silence, then the sound of Martha's heavy tread.

The sound of the dinner bell found Elly sitting on the edge of her bed. Her eyes stung, for she had been crying. But now she sat dry-eyed, paralyzed by feelings of shame, embarrassment—and a growing anger she was consciously nurturing to fight off those other two emotions.

Her gowns lay all about, draped over the bedding and the top of the trunk. She had examined them critically and was forced to admit that what Hannah had implied was true: she *did* dress like a whore. And—despite still being unsure exactly what whores did—she knew quite well that whatever it was, it was very shameful. Which was the root of her anger—for, she asked some invisible judge, what other models did she have when it came to ladies' fashions?

Applying professor Carp's methods, she had come up with a logical construct:

1. The women who work in saloons wear gowns like these.
2. Elly works in saloons. Therefore:
3. Elly should wear gowns like these.

But there was another possible construct—A. The women who work in saloons are whores, and B. Elly works in saloons—implying a different conclusion, the validity of which Elly could not deny. So that when she finally entered the dining room (wearing the dowdy, blue-checked gingham frock she wore only for breakfasting and practicing), she could hardly look at anyone, least of all Bill and Hannah.

Jimmy was finishing the story of their unsuccessful quest.

"So yer got 'im to talk to ya, did ya?" joked the Englishman.

"Uh-huh," said Jimmy, not elaborating. Elly suspected this was to spare her feelings, but since she sat on the side of Jimmy's face with the eye patch, she wasn't sure.

"He's a peculiar one, all right," said Pinky. Elly groaned inwardly at the hateful word. Hannah finished serving out some kind of meat pie and conversation ceased. As usual the food was good, but Elly hardly tasted it, concentrating instead on what she had decided to do. It would take all the courage she could muster, much more than playing for a thousand people...

There was Brown Betty for dessert, then—as though stretching its limbs after a long nap—the conversation slowly reawoke. Somebody teased Eli, the young man with the sparse beard and gold-rimmed spectacles, suggesting that any day now he would be heading back to Yale University with his tail between his legs.

"Yeah," agreed Pinky, the bearded old gnome, "must be a lark, play-actin at minin, and all the time knowin a nest of debutantes and a nice soft job in Daddy's firm are waitin for ya when you've had a belly-full."

Eli must have received such jests often, for he laughed good-naturedly.

"Ven da vinter she come," suggested the chinless Scandanavian, "I reckon dat'll chase him away all right."

The Englishman, whose name was Harold Baxter, commented on the unseasonably cold nights. "Should've brought me hot water bottle across the pond with me." He grinned toothily.

"Snowed six inches on the Fourth of July back in ninety-seven," said Pinky, who seemed to have been in Cripple Creek the longest. This led to someone asking what was on the program this year for the Fourth of July picnic. Elly feared this might be the opening volley of a lengthy conversational campaign. She took a deep breath.

"Jimmy," she said.

It came out much louder than she intended and struck the entire table dumb. Jimmy jumped in his seat as though bitten by a snake.

"Jimmy," repeated Elly, "I want to work again."

"Huh, uh, huh, yeah," mumbled Jimmy. His head was twisted far to the side so his eye could stare at Elly. Which it was doing.

"What kind of work do you do?" asked Eli, smiling at Elly in a friendly way. Which was good, because she was now so terrified, she could hardly have continued otherwise.

"I work in saloons," she said. And—turning her head and trying with all her might to look Hannah in the eye—added: "Playing the piano."

"The PIANO!" barked Hannah. One of her big hands flew to the side of her face, and she began to turn pink.

Bill Wynn glanced at her and raised an eyebrow.

"Well hey now," said Jimmy, and Elly cheered inwardly, for she could tell from the sound of his voice that the old Jimmy—the old smooth Jimmy who had disappeared during the search for Liddie—was back. "Hey now, you're lookin at the world's greatest girl pianer player. Ain't nobody can touch her. Knows ever durn song ever wrote an plays circles round folks outweighs her three-to-one. Played ever durn city in the country, an she's took em all by storm."

Bill Wynn was quietly chuckling. Hannah cast a comically mortified glance in his direction.

A jowly miner who seldom spoke leaned back in his chair, a wad of tobacco in his cheek. "Hell of a spiel," he said and spat in the brass cuspidor in the corner.

"In fact," said Elly—struggling to modulate her voice the way her father used to, when introducing her on stage (which she could only do by imagining the words forming not a sentence but a song)—"in fact, I am the one and only protégé of the great Ignatz Paderewski."

Eli exploded in helpless laughter. "Can you," he finally sputtered, "can you play the 'Minute Waltz'?"

"Hell," said Jimmy, "she can play er in forty seconds flat! An what's more"—he reached in his pocket and slapped a gold coin on the table—"I'll bet five dollar on it."

Elly was touched by this display of faith, for she was sure Jimmy had neither heard, nor heard of, the "Minute Waltz."

"Well now, Eli," said Harold Baxter, "seein as you are the one 'as challenged the little lady, I'd say you ought to put up."

There was general japing agreement, and Eli accepted the wager. Coffee was quickly drained, and there was an excited exodus saloonward.

As everyone went for their coats, Elly heard Bill Wynn's voice behind her:

"Hannah, well, this I gotta see."

After a long pause, Hannah answered: "Oh Lord, Bill—me too!"

·   ·   ·

"Elly," hissed Jimmy, as the two of them forged ahead of the boisterous throng and out of earshot, "holy jumpin turnips, Elly—jus ever time I think I knows yer, it's like yez a whole different person."

"She thought I was a whore."

"What?! Who?"

"Hannah."

"Well, why'd she think a fool thing like that?"

But Elly was talked out and only frowned and shook her head.

They arrived at the saloon where they had heard the colored piano player that first night.

Elly divided piano players into two camps: those who found the young girl who could play circles around them embodied all their worst nightmares of being upstaged, and those who delighted in her talent. Curiously, it was the better players who dominated this second group, and this man was one of the best she'd ever heard. As Jimmy swaggered toward the bar (yes, the old Jimmy was back!) she listened, fascinated, as the nattily-dressed Negro ragged the melody of "Camptown Races" in a way that made it entirely new. Behind her, she heard a coin slapped on the bar and Jimmy's boastful voice:

"Betcha this little girl here can outplay that old darkie—outplay anyone you ever heard, anywhere, anyhow."

The song ended to scattered applause from the half-filled saloon. The group from the boarding house was spilling in the doorway.

The bartender looked at Elly, then eyed the twenty-dollar gold piece on the bar. "Hey Sam," he called out, "let this little girl here play a tune."

The miners from the boarding house whooped and began moving toward two empty tables close to the piano. Sam rather bemusedly yielded the piano bench to Elly.

"Better watch out," said Eli, grinning at him. "This girl's the protégé of the great Paderewski himself!"

"That a fact?" said Sam, smiling uncertainly.

"That's right, boy," said the jowly miner, "better be careful she don't snatch up your job."

"I surely will, Cap'n, yes I surely will."

Hannah was standing and looking around with wide, scandalized eyes, and Elly knew at once she'd never been inside a saloon in her life. Bill pulled out a chair for her. She sat primly and smiled at Elly in an encouraging way, as if she were the mother of a nervous child in a school pageant. Elly squeezed her hands together, stretching her fingers, and smiled to herself.

This was the easy part.

Nobody thought to time the "Minute Waltz." For something about the whole situation seemed to fuel Elly's uncanny abilities, and the piece flew from her fingers in cascades of pearly notes at such an astonishing clip that the entire saloon was instantly spellbound. As inured to applause as she had become, the feverish response that erupted at the last chord almost made her jump. In the midst of the tumult, she watched Eli accost Jimmy and make a ceremony of paying him his five dollars as the others laughed. Sam leaned against the piano, grinning at her and shaking his head, and she knew she'd been right: he was one of the nice ones.

The bartender had wandered over. Frowning, he asked Elly if she could play any "regular" music. Realizing Jimmy's twenty dollars were still on the line, she launched into a medley of minstrel tunes that never failed to knock them dead. In her exalted state she played as if possessed, and on a whim, tacked on her own arrangement of "The Stars and Stripes Forever," thundering out the trombone part in bass octaves and managing in the final strain to combine both the glorious melody and piccolo *obbligato* in one hand. When she finished, the room was in an uproar. She heard Eli shouting that she was "a veritable phenomenon!" and watched the bartender shake his head disgustedly—then pay up.

The wild night had only just begun. Elly and Sam took turns, trading songs. People clapped, cheered, danced, sang along. And through it all, one person led the applause, clapping louder than anyone else with her big red hands.

And smiling at Elly with tears in her eyes.

Chapter Three
The Fourth of July

"Well now, Miss Elly," said Sam, pushing his derby back to scratch his head, "I surely don't know how I does it, raggin songs that way. I jus kinda feels it, like."

At the end of that wonderful night, Sam had invited Elly to return the following afternoon so they could "trade licks." She found him in his shirtsleeves, but still wearing his bowler. At her approach, he smiled and nodded but continued playing a ragtime rendition of "Beautiful Doll." She stood next to him, listening intently. For there was something in Sam's playing that was new to her, something that she was determined to understand.

Then Sam insisted she play, and she sat down and happily lost herself in a Beethoven sonata. Sam stared at her hands as they chased each other around the keyboard like twin acrobats.

"Old Sam couldn't play like that if he practiced a zillion years," he announced at the conclusion, chuckling. "And you can take that to the bank!"

"But...but I can't rag a song like you can," countered Elly.

That's when Sam tried to explain. But when there seemed no words for what he was trying to communicate, he shrugged and taking the bench again, plunged into "Swanee River" in a slow strut. He ripped the melody with a roll of his right hand, adding extra notes with his thumb, while rocking out the beat with his left hand, relaxed and steady.

He played through a chorus and jumped up from the piano. "Now you do it."

Elly leapt onto the bench and copied him.

"Ha, uh-huh, yass!" cried Sam, laughing and slapping his knee. "It's perfect, yes indeed, it's *zackly* like old Sam played it, and that's a fact. Only, only"—he scratched his head again and revealed the bald spot his derby was hiding—"maybe a little *too* zackly."

Elly looked up at him, perplexed.

"What old Sam means to say is—well, if you does it the same way every time, you ain't really doin it."

Elly was still confused.

"Well, let's see now," said Sam, gently pushing Elly aside, "maybe I can…"

He played the same song again, but this time ragged it in a manner entirely different. "You see, Miss Elly? Is you absorbin what old Sam be tryin to tell you?"

Elly nodded slowly, a gleam in her eyes.

That evening at dinner, the talk was of the Elks Lodge dance on the Fourth of July, which most of the miners would be attending as Bill Wynn's guests. All during dinner, Hannah had seemed tongue-tied in a manner quite unlike her, and Elly suspected she was still embarrassed by her earlier suspicions. Finally she spoke up, insisting that Jimmy and Elly attend the dance as well, and looked almost pathetically grateful when Elly nodded her acceptance. Once again, Elly bemoaned her inability to speak—when a happy thought occurred to her.

"Would you," she asked Hannah, "would you help me choose a new dress?"

Hannah's long jaw dropped—then she clapped her hands and said "YES!" so loudly that Martha dropped the pie tins she was clearing away. A few minutes later, Hannah and Elly were huddled together at the kitchen table over the latest Montgomery Ward catalogue like co-conspirators while Martha grumbled over the dishes. And the following day, Hannah whisked Elly off to Smeltzer's Fine Dressmaking.

Nellie Smeltzer was a corpulent woman with traces of a former beauty still visible in her face, like the blurred outlines in the sand of some ancient, buried palace. Elly stood and allowed herself to be measured. With a thrill she imagined how a bride must feel being fitted for her wedding gown (though the large woman's hands roving over her body gave her a strange feeling).

They decided on a gown of maroon velvet with puffed sleeves and trimmed with black silk ribbons. As they walked back to the boarding house, Hannah reminisced about the dress she had worn to her own very first dance.

"It was when Henry and I—my husband—were first sparking. So young we were! Just fifteen, the both of us. My dress was velvet too, but blue—midnight blue. Which was about the time I got home—ha!—and found out my father had locked the door on me. Well, I just went straight out to the woodshed and got the axe. Chopped a panel out of that door—swinging the axe in my blue velvet dress!—and let myself in. Next day, Daddy replaced that panel but never said a word. Fact, neither of us ever mentioned it—ha!"

A couple of days later, Jimmy was grousing to Elly about his roommate, Zachary Crabbe.

"Snores, farts in his sleep, an ain't got a word to say fer hisself. Like livin with a ghost what stinks an hogs the blankets."

They were following behind old Sam, who was again proving himself quite the best sort of pianist by casting all thoughts of rivalry aside and taking Elly around to where a "sugarplum of a job, yessir, a regular goldmine, pardon the expression" had just opened up at an establishment by the name of Crapper Jack's Saloon and Dance Hall.

"If it's such a hell-firin great job, why didn't yer take it yourself?" said Jimmy.

Old Sam looked rather hurt. "Well, cause I give my word to play out the season where I am. And once old Sam Hackett give his word, that's the end of it, yessir. And you can take that to the bank."

Elly frowned at Jimmy, who shrugged.

"But when the summer ends, it's back to Little Rock for old Sam," continued their guide, as he led them down a street crowded with saloons and cafés and dance halls. "Cause Ol Man Winter, he come early up here, an he come hard. Yessir, I seen one Cripple Creek winter, and that's enough for old Sam…"

Crapper Jack's Saloon and Dance Hall was a long, narrow room with a low tin ceiling and a mirrored bar running its entire length. An upright piano sat on a stage at the rear. In front of the stage was a large area big enough for thirty dancing couples. A few men sat drinking at the bar, but in the early afternoon, the place was mostly empty. Crapper Jack himself, a burly, bearded man with small sharp eyes, emerged from a back office chewing an unlit cigar. Old Sam began talking Elly up.

Crapper Jack stared at her skeptically, then interrupted Sam's spiel to ask, "Just how the fuck old is she, anyways?"

"Jus turned sixteen," said Jimmy quickly. It was the lie they'd started telling ever since Elly had grown tall.

Crapper Jack's piggish eyes narrowed into slits. He chewed his cigar. Finally he waved a fat hand toward the stage. "Play somethin."

Ten minutes later Elly was perspiring, the men at the bar were loudly applauding, and Crapper Jack had gone from skeptic to believer. "Four dollars a night," he said. "Seven to twelve. Ten minute breaks."

"Now Cap'n," said Sam, "you know she's worth more than that."

"She'll make most of her money in tips."

"Yessir, she surely will," agreed Sam, smiling. But he stood his ground.

Jimmy looked on approvingly. There was a silence. Crapper Jack's unlit cigar twitched up and down. "Six," he said.

"And fifteen minute breaks."

"Nope. No can do."

Sam turned to Elly with a long face. "Miss Elly, I'm just so sorry I done wasted your time here—"

Crapper Jack threw up his arms. "All right all right, you win."

"But," said Elly, "I can't start until after the Fourth of July."

Crapper Jack chewed his cigar a very long time before pulling it from his mouth and stabbing old Sam in the chest with it. "She better be worth the wait."

He stomped away.

Elly's new job confirmed her celebrity status to the patrons of Hannah Moffet's boarding house, if not to the proprietress herself.

"Crapper Jack's!" she exclaimed when Jimmy announced the news at dinner. "Isn't that place rather—well, rather notorious?"

"That's the word for it, all right!" agreed Pinky with enthusiasm.

"Well, um," murmured Bill Wynn, "they say it *can* get rather boisterous there on occasion—"

"I 'eard when Rheinhart struck it at the Lucky Gus," grinned Harold Baxter, displaying his spectacularly crooked teeth, "he stood treat for a hundred people and danced a polka in 'is union suit."

"But the women there," said Hannah doubtfully, "the ones who dance with the men—"

"For a dime," said Eli, grinning.

"*I* should get a job there," said Martha. She slung three blueberry pies on the table, then did a clumsy little shimmy.

"Martha, that dance ain't worth two cents," said Pinky.

"Oh *pshh*!" said Martha, slapping at him.

"Them girls'll do other stuff too," said Jake, the jowly miner whose mouth was always stuffed with either food or tobacco. He leered around the table.

Zachary Crabbe raised his pimply face from his plate to snicker. He was an uncommonly homely youth, with a nose that started one direction then changed its mind, and long, goatish teeth.

"Cept," continued Jake, "*that'll* cost ya more'n ten—"

He broke off at the sight of Hannah's face.

Jimmy took in her expression as well. "Hey now," he said "you don't have to worry bout ol Elly. I'll be there ever minute, an anyone tries any monkey business, well—"

He reached inside a vest pocket and whipped out his derringer with a theatrical air.

"Jimmy," said Hannah matter-of-factly, "I do not allow firearms at the dinner table." She stared at him.

Jimmy mumbled "Yes'm," and slipped it back in his pocket.

Hannah nodded and began to slice the pies. Elly couldn't help but notice that she served Bill Wynn the biggest piece.

Elly speculated endlessly on Bill and Hannah's relationship. They had a nightly ritual of drinking tea together at the kitchen table, and she could hear their conversations (or rather Hannah's monologues and Bill's murmured interjections) through her wall. As far as she could tell though, Bill was always the perfect gentleman, and there was a disappointing scarcity of romantic heat between them.

But in the most secret recesses of her heart, Elly was happy about this. Because it made it easier, when Bill turned his pale blue eyes in her direction, to imagine it was her—Elly—he was in love with.

"But, but, I don't *want* to be a rose," declared Moosie, pouting. "I want to be a, a *squirrel*."

"If you don't stop fidgeting, you're not going to be anything at all," said Hannah.

She fiddled once more with the chicken wire framing Moosie's stubborn face, then turned to Elly. "What do you think?"

The chicken wire was draped with pink muslin and, in combination with Moosie's green cotton frock, was supposed to transform her into a rose bloom. With other similarly attired little girls, she was to ride on a float in tomorrow's Fourth of July parade and toss free samples of Pear's flower-scented soap into the crowd.

Elly thought Moosie looked less like a rose than a little girl whose head had been swallowed by a pink comforter, but she nodded encouragingly.

"Squirrels can climb, can climb trees!" cried Moosie, jerking from her mother's grasp and miming enthusiastic climbing motions, causing the chicken wire bloom to pop from her head like an exploding pink halo.

"Oh Lord," cried Hannah, casting her eyes to the ceiling, "give me strength!"

Elly decided this was a very good time to slip out the front door and head to Smithson's Machine Shop.

~~~

She found Lucas Cornwall squatting in a corner, wearing a pair of tinted goggles, and directing a blue-orange jet of gas flame at a skeletal metal assembly. Sparks danced crazily around him. He acknowledged Elly's presence by standing, rummaging around a work table, wordlessly handing her a shard of smoky glass, then returning to his work. Holding the glass up to her eyes, Elly could discern how the metal rod Lucas held in his gloved hand, under steady, precise motions of the flame, was somehow fusing the assembly together.

He worked for a long time as though she wasn't there. Once a pot-bellied man in greasy corduroys ambled over and asked, "She botherin ya, Lucas?"

Lucas shook his head without looking at him.

The man nodded amiably and ambled away.

Finally Lucas closed the valve on the gas tank and pushed up his goggles.

"Frame," he said. "For a hoist."

Elly divined from his manner that this was nothing very exciting. She nodded.

Lucas picked up a hammer and, with sudden manic energy, began pounding on the new joints—testing them, Elly guessed. Apparently satisfied, he put the hammer down and walked toward a pair of huge double doors on the side of the building. Elly followed him. In front of the doors rested something very large, covered with a canvas tarp. Lucas carefully pulled it aside and revealed a long, gleaming motorcar, forest green with brass trim.

He turned his pale face toward Elly.

"Pierce-Arrow."

Elly gazed at it, rapt.

He released a catch, lifted one side of the metal housing covering the front of the car, and together they peered inside. Nestled in the space, like a powerful genie inside his lamp, was the engine. Lucas raised an enquiring eyebrow at her.

"It's beautiful," she murmured.

The edges of Lucas's mouth subtly twitched, and Elly recognized it as her own kind of smile. Suddenly he began to spout words.

"In-line six cylinder," he intoned, in his strange, flat voice, so like hers. "Five inch bore, seven inch stroke. Makes a bore/stroke ratio of point seven one. Two valves per cylinder. Four speed gearbox. Sixty horsepower…"

Though she only dimly understood the words, they had a kind of poetry, and Elly memorized them all. The fount of statistics flowed on in a steady stream, then abruptly ceased. There was a long pause, the kind Elly recognized only too well. And she knew Lucas was planning the next thing he was going to say.

"Do you," he said finally, staring off to one side, "do you want to learn?"

Elly nodded.

Lucas nodded as well. For the first time he looked directly at her. "You'll get dirty," he said.

Elly shrugged.

There was a strange, snuffling noise: Lucas laughing.

"Okay," he said.

Four hours later, Elly emerged from the cryptlike depths of the machine shop into bright sunlight, blinking. It had just rained—one of the brief showers that seemed to come every afternoon at the same time—and the gravel beneath her feet glistened. A glint of color caught her eye, and she bent to pick up a shiny blue-green stone.

A rainbow arched over the crest of a nearby hill, and on a whim, she decided to follow it. With each step, the thrilling new words ran through her head—piston, crankshaft, carburetor, spark plug, valve, gasket, magneto—together with the precious knowledge of how they all worked together to make power. The power of sixty horses...

She reached the top and caught her breath. Mountains pale pink as seashells, so distant they might have been dreams, ringed the horizon. The town lay beneath her like wooden blocks carelessly scattered by a child. She looked again at the stone in her hand—yes, it had to be a piece of turquoise—then held her arms out. The pine-scented breeze blew her frock against her body and cooled her hot forehead. She felt so full of life she could have screamed, grown feathers and flown, spontaneously combusted...

But none of these things occurred, so instead she returned to the boarding house.

Hannah was in the kitchen preparing to bake raspberry cakes for tomorrow's Elks Lodge dance. She took one look at the oil-stained ruin that had been Elly's gingham frock, gave her a scolding, then rummaged around and handed her an old patched pair of miner's overalls.

"There. In case you ever have another hare-brained hankering to become a grease-monkey."

Elly took the overalls, smiling to herself, for nothing could alter her mood. She cleaned herself up, donned the overalls (which made her look like a scarecrow, she thought), tied her damp hair back, and—by way of atonement (and even though she knew nothing whatever about baking)—offered to help Hannah with her cakes.

"Sweet of you," said Hannah. "Martha's off trying to finish sewing her frock for the dance. Though how it will turn out, well the Lord only knows," she added. She worked as she chatted, and Elly had a sense of what others felt watching her play the piano, for Hannah's hands were everywhere at once—sifting, stirring, pulling things from cupboards, tasting, testing the oven—all the time setting small tasks for Elly and monitoring her progress. "Girl can hardly sew a lick, but how can you blame her? The poor thing lost her father in the depot explosion, one of those scab miners—oh, but you know nothing about those terrible times. There was an epidemic of pneumonia that year, and her mother died soon after. If I hadn't taken her on, well, there's no telling what might have become of her."

Hannah sniffed, somehow suggesting she knew very well just what would have become of Martha. As she chattered on, Elly filed away these references to a depot explosion and "scab miners" as further clues. For she was certain now there was some mystery about Cripple Creek, some terrible occurrence in the not-so-distant past. Chance remarks at the dinner table. The joke Pinky made about starting "a new union, a union of geezers," which had fallen flat and caused Bill to change the subject. The uncomfortable silence that had descended on the table when Eli asked Bill if he "actually *knew* Harry Orchard." This time it was Hannah who had brightly asked if anyone wanted more pie. But not before Elly noted Bill's reluctant nod of assent.

All this excited Elly, because she was now completely in thrall to the mysteries of Sherlock Holmes. She delighted in the way the master detective used the same sort of logic Professor Carp had taught her to solve the devilishly ingenious puzzles that confronted him with miraculous frequency, and longed for a mystery to solve herself. And now it seemed she had not one but two, for surely Liddie's disappearance counted as a perfect mystery!

With such thoughts swirling through her mind, she paid little attention to the cake pans she was supposed to be greasing.

"Lord, not that thick!" clucked Hannah. "We're not *frying* them!"

They poured the batter into the pans, set the cakes to baking, and made a frosting of butter, sugar, and red food coloring. When the cakes were done and had cooled, they mortared the layers with frosting, slathered the result in yet more frosting, then studded them with wild raspberries. Hannah rolled her eyes at Elly's compulsion to arrange her raspberries in perfectly symmetrical patterns and finished five cakes before Elly half-completed one. Moosie materialized just in time to lick the icing bowl (getting more icing on her face and in her hair than in her mouth). Finally she flashed her mother an impish look, snatched a raspberry from atop a cake, popped it in her mouth, and skipped away.

Hannah pretended annoyance. But a few minutes later, as the two of them sat at the kitchen table over cups of tea, she sighed.

"Lord, Elly. Sometimes…sometimes when that child looks at me like that, those green eyes full of devilment, well…my heart just melts." Hannah turned her own big gray eyes on Elly. "Because…because they're Henry's—my husband's—eyes. And that's exactly the way he used to look at me."

Hannah had begun to confide in Elly (as people had her entire life, knowing she would tell no tales). Elly was thrilled by this development, for she had lived so long amongst men that Hannah's confidences came as exciting bulletins from a foreign country called Womanhood. A place she now found herself steaming toward, eyes eagerly scanning the horizon for a landfall.

She sipped her tea and waited.

"Lord," continued Hannah, "when that man looked at me like that…well, he could do just about anything he wanted with me." Hannah's face flushed. She took another sip of tea. "Not that he was perfect. I mean, he was a *man*. Someday you'll find out what that means." She gave a small chuckle, then sighed. "What Moosie sorely needs is a father. And that poor man never even got to see his own daughter."

It seemed an invitation to ask the question Elly had long wanted to ask. She cleared her throat.

"What...what happened to him?"

Hannah glanced at her, then looked into her tea cup as though she might read the answer in the bottom like some gypsy fortune teller.

Elly waited.

"What happened was, I got a knock on my door in the middle of the night. And that's a sound you never want to hear when your husband is working the night shift. So I threw on my robe and waddled to the door—I was already big with Moosie—and there were ten or twelve miners and him not among them, and I knew already. They all came inside and took their hats off, and one of them started building up the fire because it was January and the cabin was deathly cold. And I asked them, 'How bad is he hurt?' and they said it was pretty bad. So I said, 'Well then I have to go to him.' Then they told me he had drilled into a hole filled with powder that hadn't gone off and was torn to pieces, and he was dead. And I just crumpled up right there on the floor."

Elly was appalled by Hannah's tragic tale, and tried to think what to say.

"That's all right," said Hannah. She reached over and squeezed Elly's hand. "There's nothing one *can* say, is there? Just nothing at all a body can say."

She stood and began to bustle about, cleaning the kitchen.

The Fourth of July dawned and found the boarding house transformed into a madhouse. The men who were to march yelled for help with their outfits, and Hannah ran around with a mouth full of pins.

Moosie was everywhere underfoot and in tears because she did not yet have her costume on. When Elly finally helped her into it, the child raced giddily around the house, her bloom became misshapen and bedraggled, and she was soon in tears again because now she "didn't look like a rose at all…"

They were running late and had to race through the town. Bill Wynn carried the wilted and tear-stained Moosie in his arms. The parade was already formed and about to get underway. Bill handed Moosie up to the Pear's Soap float, then ran off to find his brother Elks. Moosie was given a basket full of soaps and immediately began flinging them from the still-stationary float with giddy abandon.

"Oh Lord," said Hannah, "they'll be gone before they even start moving…"

Hannah, Jimmy, Elly, and Martha hurried back through the town to find a spot to watch the parade. The streets were thronged with people, the town swollen to twice its size by visitors from Colorado Springs up on the morning train. The parade appeared down the street and was led, to Elly's amazement, by the same Pierce-Arrow whose valves she had helped Lucas adjust the day before; it was like seeing a man who'd just been on the operating table get up and walk around. A goggled chauffeur was at the wheel, and a fat man in a silk top hat sat in back waving regally to the crowd.

"That's Charlie Tutt," said Hannah. "Owns the richest mine in Cripple Creek."

Two marching bands in gaudy finery followed, playing with more enthusiasm than skill. The music of both bands was jumbled together, with a discordant result suggestive of clashing armies. A battalion of miners marched behind them, boots and helmets scrubbed and polished, carrying their picks over their shoulders like rifles. Floats began to appear, including a gaily-colored number topped by a bouquet of whimsically-attired little girls. One of them had an empty basket, drooping petals, and pouting face—which burst into sunny smiles when she spotted them waving at her. Interspersed with the floats marched the various fraternal orders, with their fezzes, their glittering scabbards, the Elks in royal purple sashes.

Elly decided Bill Wynn was quite the handsomest Elk.

The bands were gone, but they could hear some other kind of music growing louder and louder—and now they could see, bringing up the rear of the parade, a carriage bearing a marvelous contraption belching steam from tall brass pipes. Down the street it came, the music now so loud Elly wondered if the matched white horses pulling the carriage had been specially selected for deafness. As it passed by, she saw the machine was being controlled by a dark-faced, derbied figure perched on the back and playing a tiny three-octave keyboard—Old Sam!—playing "Alexander's Ragtime Band" with such rhythmic energy that a crowd of youths were dancing the cakewalk in the street behind the carriage to form an impromptu finale to the parade.

Jimmy, Elly, and Martha looked at one another—then rushed out into the street to join them.

The afternoon was a confusion of sights, smells, sounds, tastes. Greasy, grilled bratwurst on rolls dripping with mustard and sauerkraut (though Elly ate hers plain). Jake from the boardinghouse, stripped to the waist and gleaming with perspiration, standing on a raised platform in front of a big crowd and swinging his hammer at a monstrous rock, as his partner rotated the drill between each powerful stroke. Martha leaning on Jimmy's shoulder while he tried to hit the scowling face of a cut-out Indian with a rubber ball, Jimmy cursing each time he missed. A crowd of people waltzing in the street to a German band playing "The Artist's Life," watched impassively by a group of swarthy men with dark mustaches and women with their hair up in kerchiefs. And Moosie, her face sticky with cotton candy, going round and round on a merry-go-round endlessly playing "Daddy Wouldn't Buy Me a Bow-wow, Bow-wow..."

They got back in just in time to help make the ice cream—from ice, Elly was told, which had been chopped from a frozen puddle at the bottom of a mine shaft—taking turns at cranking the stiff handle. Everything else was ready, and Elly had just time to change into her new frock and get Hannah to attach a matching maroon velvet bow to her hair.

"Oh Elly," she gushed, "you're just a little heartbreaker!"

Elly blushed—then blushed again when Bill Wynn helped her into her coat and murmured that she looked "real pretty." They set off for the Elks Lodge with two buckets of ice cream and six carefully-boxed cakes. It was already dark and once again cold, but the downtown was alive with revelers. Chinese lanterns swung gaily above the main streets. Laughter and drunken singing were punctuated by distant gunshots. They climbed an outside stairway to the second story of a brick building and were met at the door by a blast of warm air and the sounds of fiddle music and stomping feet. By the time they shed their coats and added the food to a long table overloaded with cakes, pies, and punch, the tune had ended, and the caller was announcing something called a "Prairie Queen." Elly watched Bill Wynn steer Hannah toward the dance floor. The way his hand rested on the small of Hannah's back gave Elly a queer thrill.

The fiddler struck up the rhythm, and the rest of the band (including, Elly noticed, a rather ham-fisted piano player) joined in. The caller cried out in a piercing tenor:

Gents to the right:
Swing the one that looks so sweet,
Now the one that dresses neat,
Now the one with the little feet,
Now the belle of the ball—room!

Ladies to the right:
Swing the one that looks so shy,
Then the one with the red necktie,

Now the one that kicks so high,
Now the best in the ball—room!"

Hannah and Bill had made the rounds of partners and were back together. They were the same height—with her long hair piled atop her head, Hannah was even a bit taller—and she gazed straight into Bill's eyes, flushed, smiling, her ungainly body rendered somehow beautiful, thought Elly, by her graceful footwork and the exalted expression on her face.

"Hain't never seen a woman so mashed on a gent," said Harold Baxter.

"He's a stone fool not to marry her," said Pinky. "Woman can bake like she does."

"'e would, you know. But he's a proud one, the Gov'ner. Won't do it till he can make the Cresson pay."

"Well then," said Pinky, disgusted, "she's doomed to be a widder for life."

The song ended. Hannah curtsied to Bill with a mocking smile, he bowed deeply in reply, and they strolled arm and arm toward the dessert table. Elly followed behind them (she had lost neither her skill at—nor taste for—eavesdropping), but Hannah only began to gossip about people Elly didn't know. So she took a plate and served herself a piece of the raspberry cake she had helped bake, topped by a scoop of the ice cream she had helped churn. The band struck up a polka, but (absorbed in making sure each bite contained exactly one raspberry and the perfect proportion of ice cream) she paid little attention. So she was taken by surprise when the music ended and the caller suddenly announced:

"Ladies and gents, we have a very special guest here tonight, a little lady who, I'm told, is just a first-class piano player—"

Elly looked up, startled, her mouth full of cake.

"—that's her over there, her name's Elly, and I bet if we just give her a little encouragement…"

People began to applaud. Elly saw Jimmy and Eli standing beside the caller, Jimmy smirking in her direction. Hannah and Bill had come up next to her, urging her on. Mildly irked (but secretly rather pleased), she handed her plate to Hannah and made her way to the stage. The piano player, a bearded man in red suspenders, grudgingly yielded the bench to her.

On a whim, she plunged into "Alexander's Ragtime Band," doing her best to apply Sam's lessons, rocking out a steady beat and elaborating on the melody. When she finished there were whoops, and she realized a crowd of younger people had been cakewalking to the music. But the rest of her audience appeared somewhat bemused, and their applause was merely polite.

Then Eli leaned over and suggested she play "The Stars and Stripes Forever."

At the sound of that first strutting phrase an electric current seemed to sweep through the crowd, and this time she brought the house down. But the cries for "More!" were overwhelmed by the news that the fireworks were starting, and there was a rush for the door. Elly followed behind, avoiding anyone who looked ready to compliment her; she would rather play a hundred Sousa marches than be fussed over for five minutes. She stood with the rest of the crowd in the refreshingly cold air and watched the display. And decided that—though the fireworks were nice—no roman candle or bursting flower basket could compete with a sky already so gloriously strewn with stars.

They all trooped back upstairs, and the caller shouted out it was time for a waltz. Elly watched with amusement as Martha tried to drag Jimmy out onto the dance floor, him resisting as one might resist being dragged toward a snake pit—when she realized Bill Wynn was smiling down at her.

"Miss Elly, may I have the pleasure?"

She wanted to melt, to run away, to die on the spot. But she made the mistake of looking directly into Bill's china-blue eyes, and the next instant found herself being led to the dance floor like a lamb to the slaughter. He put an arm around her waist and lifted her hand to his shoulder. The music started up, her heart was beating like mad, she was shaking her head no, no—

"Don't worry," Bill murmured into her ear, "I'll teach you. As much music as you have inside you, well…"

And then she was being whirled around. And was suddenly aware that, in all her fantasies of what it might be like to waltz, she had never considered *feet*—and hers were moving so ineptly. Then a moment later she had forgotten all that, aware only of Bill's hand on her waist, the warmth and strength of his body, the lights moving around them in circles, and the waltz, the lovely "Merry Widow Waltz." And knew that, for the rest of her life, it would ever sound the same…

Suddenly it was over, and Bill was bowing to her. She made a clumsy (*so* clumsy!) attempt at a curtsey, then walked away and stood against the wall, trying to take in what had just happened, to remember every second so she would never forget—then saw Hannah beaming at her maternally from across the room and wanted to die all over again. She drifted over to where Bill was now standing with Harold Baxter and a group of men she didn't know and found a good spot for eavesdropping, both afraid—and secretly hoping—they might be teasing him about their dance.

But it was just more mining talk.

"I hear Lewis is makin Badger Boy pay," said one.

"Time he pays expenses, don't see how he can even break even, ore that low-grade," said another.

"I'll tell ya how," said a third. "It's all them hunkies and dagoes he's got on the job."

"You've struck it there. That's one thing you can say for the Federation—they never stood for hiring that sort."

"They're good workers," said Bill mildly, speaking for the first time.

"The Gov'ner's right," agreed Harold Baxter. "Though the lunches they pack do smell peculiar."

"Say, that's right Bill—heard you got a whole pack of em on your payroll."

"Bill, even you fill the Cresson with chinks, you'll never make that dud pay."

The men chuckled.

"Still say things would be better if we could get the union back."

"You're wishin for the moon. Federation cut its own throat when they blew up the depot and killed all them scabs."

"Wasn't the Federation that hired Harry Orchard," said a hard-faced man with graying greased-back hair.

There was an uncomfortable silence. Elly was paying close attention now.

"You believe that old rumor?" said someone finally.

"Orchard made a full confession," said someone else, agreeing. "After that business up in Idaho. Admitted it was all his own idea."

"Orchard was a plant," shot back the man with greased hair. "A Pinkerton spy. Mine owners planned the whole thing to discredit the Federation."

"Talk like that ain't safe, and you know it," muttered someone.

"Even so, it's the truth. There was a witness—"

"Says you," said the other, raising his voice.

"Boys," interrupted Bill, "it's seven years ago now, all this. Time to forget and move on."

"But I tell you there was a witness," repeated the man stubbornly. "But the mine owners had him killed."

"Guess there ain't no witness now," scoffed someone.

Once again there was a silence. Carefully Elly filed away all these new clues to the mystery.

"Looks like young Jimmy's got 'is 'ands full," observed Harold Baxter.

Elly looked and saw Jimmy being pulled by Martha around the dance floor, and looking about as enthusiastic as a dog being bathed. The men appeared happy to have the subject changed and chuckled.

"He one of your boys, Bill?" asked someone.

"Jimmy? No, he's here looking for his sister, Liddie. Liddie Skeets. Came here four or five years ago, stayed in Hannah's boarding house for a spell. Before my time."

"Liddie," said someone. "I remember a Liddie. Pretty little thing? Kinda brownish-blondish hair?"

"I believe Hannah said it was," replied Bill.

"Sure, Liddie. Oh, she was a little firecracker, all right. Worked at Minnie Smith's place. Ain't seen her in a couple a years, though."

Elly held her breath.

"Well," said Bill, "I suppose that must have been her. But for God's sake, don't tell the boy his sister became a whore."

The caller announced the last dance, the "Home Sweet Home Waltz," and the men broke up to find their wives and sweethearts. Elly watched Hannah smile broadly as Bill strode toward her. Martha was trying to coax Jimmy out again, but he lounged against a wall with his arms crossed and shook his head with smirking finality. While Elly stood and brooded, realizing she had finally begun to solve both mysteries.

And wishing she hadn't.

Chapter Four

Crapper Jack's

Elly found playing in a dance hall to be a fascinating—if rather exhausting—experience.

It wasn't at all like playing in a saloon for a few people gathered around the piano, where she could alternate her more athletic showpieces with sentimental ballads. Now every song had to be charged with rhythm to coax people on to the dance floor. But it was wonderfully exciting, the way the intensity of her own feelings for the waltzes, polkas, and rags that she played seemed to flow from her fingers into the feet of the people dancing. It was as though they were puppets, and she pulling the strings.

And then there were the women.

In the saloons where she had played, there might have been three or four. Here there were twenty-five or thirty. Dressed relatively modestly, in white cotton frocks and black stockings. And all of them depending on her to get the men up and buying dances from them—depending on Elly to help them make a living.

She was made painfully aware of this her very first night. She had opened with what she thought a very good "Blue Danube"—with all its lovely languorous subthemes and exciting coda—only to have a rather hard-faced woman break off from her partner at the end to hiss at her:

"Whatcha tryin a do? Makin us dance a dollar's worth for a dime!"

The dancers shuffled tiredly off the floor, some of them flashing Elly dirty looks. For two bits, the men got a dance and a shot of whiskey, and they were lining up at the bar. The woman who had complained was leaning over the bar talking to Crapper Jack and pointing at Elly accusingly. A table full of men from the boarding house had come for her opening night and were clapping like mad, but Elly, mortified, paid no attention.

Curly (a huge, moon-faced man who doubled as bouncer and emcee) announced the next dance. This time she brought the rag she was playing to an early finish and glanced at the woman who had complained. She nodded grudgingly.

The men from the boarding house stayed late, whooping and leading the applause. Bill Wynn paid a short visit, flustering Elly by his very presence. But Hannah had refused to enter a place where the women earned such a questionable living.

"Lord, Elly, why must you work in such an establishment?" she had muttered that evening as Elly (again wearing her blue velvet gown) set out for Crapper Jack's. "You!" she said, fixing Jimmy with a look such as a general might give a private. "You take good care of her, you hear?"

But Elly soon discovered that the women at Crapper Jack's turned Jimmy's head to the point that he began neglecting his duties.

Chief among these had always been the job of fending off people during her breaks. Elly preferred to spend these times in a quiet corner reading, and had a terror of strangers trying to engage her in conversation. But instead of hurrying to her side when she finished her sets, Jimmy was now more likely to be found strutting about the room like a rooster in a hen house, or sitting at a distant table displaying the "giant-killer" to some impressionable young thing.

So she was forced to fend for herself, and it wasn't long before three of the women cornered her. One was the hard-faced woman who had complained. Up close, she seemed rather old and scarily mannish, and Elly was privately surprised that anyone would want to dance with her.

"Mind if we join ya, or are ya too grand for the likes of us?" she said, grinning archly as all three sat down uninvited.

"Whatcha readin?" asked a round, bland-faced young woman with brightly hennaed hair. She leaned over and squinted at the title.

"*The Return of Sherlock Holmes*," murmured Elly, blushing furiously.

"Kinda book is that?"

"Detective."

"Hmph," exclaimed the mannish woman. "Had my fill of detectives with them Pinkertons."

"Them's the ones stirred everything up, all right," agreed the other. "In the bad times."

Elly pricked up her ears, hoping they would say more on this subject, but instead they introduced themselves. The mannish woman was Mamie, the unnatural redhead was Helma, and the third was a cross-eyed girl named Iris who didn't look much older than Elly.

Iris must have been thinking the same thing. "How old are you?" she asked Elly.

"Sixteen."

"In a pig's eye," said Mamie.

"Wish I could play like you," sighed Iris. Her eyes were so skewed she might have been addressing any one of them. "Wouldn't have to shuffle round getting pawed at by stinky miners."

"You do play real pretty," agreed Helma. "Make me wanna shake my leg."

"Thank you," Elly managed to say.

There was a silence.

"Talkative sort, ain't ya?" said Helma.

Elly searched her mind desperately for a reply.

"Don't like talkin to *us*, what it is," said Mamie, pushing her chair back. "Come on, girls."

They all stood up.

"Nice to meet you, Elly," said Iris over her shoulder.

Elly nodded dumbly.

Agonizing over her difficulties making conversation, Elly had tried to analyze what it was that normal people did when they talked. And concluded that, for most people, it was a sort of game, in which banal phrases and more-or-less pointless stories are lobbed back and forth—anything to keep the conversational ball aloft. Whereas to Elly's way of thinking, a conversation was an exchange of information that, once imparted, implied no need to drag things out.

And now she had finally found another person who felt the same way.

Three or four times a week she donned her overalls and visited Lucas. He had begun to give her things to disassemble, so she could learn how to use wrenches and screwdrivers and pliers and all the other mysterious and wonderful tools strewn about the machine shop. The pot-bellied man—who Elly had learned was Mr. Smithson, the owner—had asked again if Lucas had any problem with her; Lucas had shaken his head, and that was that. And she came to realize Lucas had a rather privileged position as the only employee Mr. Smithson trusted with the delicate inner workings of the various engines that needed repair.

At first she was miserably inept, and paid for her lack of skill by playing in the evenings with skinned knuckles and bruised fingers. But Lucas was endlessly patient and left her alone to learn things for herself, occasionally offering some terse piece of advice—"Put some oil on it first"—or silently demonstrating how to use the weight of one's body to put power behind a screwdriver.

They took breaks together and on fine days would sit outside, leaning against the building. Lucas would roll and smoke a cigarette. And they would talk in the way Elly thought talking should be.

Elly: "Do you like Cripple Creek?"

Lucas: "Yes."

Silence.

Lucas: "Sometimes I go fishing."

Silence.

Elly: "Can I go fishing with you sometime?"

Lucas: "Yes."

Silence.

Such exchanges Elly found perfectly satisfying.

One afternoon, they sat together in companionable silence, watching a distant train full of ore snake down a hillside. Elly said:

"I heard some men say that Liddie became a whore."

Lucas stared at his feet. He nodded slowly.

"They said she worked at Minnie Smith's place."

Lucas considered this. "That would be one of those houses. On Myer Street."

"The place I work at is on Myer Street."

"Further down. Near the M-T Trestle."

Elly nodded.

"There are five or six of them. You can ask."

Elly nodded again. Lucas finished his cigarette. And they went back to work.

Next afternoon, she found the row of unassuming frame houses near the train trestle and knocked on the door of the first one. The colored maid who opened the door gave her a funny look, then pointed to the fourth house down.

It was a dilapidated structure, with peeling paint and incongruous red brocade curtains. This time, a heavily made-up woman in a silk kimono answered the door, laughing over her shoulder at something someone behind her had just said.

"Next time give him a belt in the puss," she retorted, eliciting another round of laughter. Finally she turned to Elly and raised an eyebrow. "I'm sorry, honey, but Minnie don't take em as young as you."

Elly felt herself blush. "I'm looking for Liddie Skeets," she said.

"Don't know her," said the woman, starting to close the door.

"Can I talk," said Elly desperately, "can I talk to Minnie?"

An older woman, her head wrapped in a crimson turban, appeared in the doorway.

"What is it, sweetie?"

"Are you Minnie Smith?"

"Uh-huh, last time I checked."

"Do you know Liddie Skeets?"

Her face changed. "Liddie? You don't mean Liddie McGann, do you?"

Of course, thought Elly—Liddie would have changed her name back. She nodded quickly.

"Well sure I knew her. She worked here for a spell. But she's been gone two years now at least."

"Where did she go?"

"Well, she left town, I know that. Beyond that, I got no idea."

Elly took a deep breath. "It's important," she said, surprising herself.

Minnie Smith hesitated, then opened the door and led her into a parlor. Two young women in sateen gowns sprawled on their stomachs on the carpet, playing cards. Both were shoeless, and their legs, clad in garish striped stockings, kicked in lazy circles; they looked like overgrown children.

"Where's Phelia?" said Minnie.

"Don't know," said one.

"Still asleep," said the other.

"Well get her," said Minnie.

The two girls stared each other down. Finally one grimaced, got sulkily to her feet, and thumped upstairs. Minnie sat on a sofa and pointed Elly to an armchair. A few minutes later, the girl returned with another in tow. Very pale and thin, wearing a silk wrapper, her blonde hair in tangles.

"What?" she said. "It's too early for me to work, after all them last night."

"Phelia, this girl is asking about Liddie."

"Liddie?" said Phelia. She regarded Elly without much interest.

"Wants to know where she went."

"How the fuck should I know?" said Phelia. She pulled at a loose strand of hair petulantly.

"Well didn't she tell you anything before she left?"

Phelia let out a histrionic sigh and shrugged. "Said she hated this place."

Minnie flashed her a look.

"Cripple, I mean. Said she might try her luck in St. Louie, New Orleans, someplace like that." She chewed her lip. "Well that's all she told me," she said defensively. "Can I go back to sleep now? After the way you worked me last night," she added, pouting.

"You didn't work no harder than me," said one of the two girls playing cards.

"Uh-huh, well you didn't have no fat men, and I got three of em. And all of em made me get on top and I bout wore myself—"

"Phelia," said Minnie, "you can go back to bed now." She glanced significantly toward Elly.

Phelia's eyes widened—then her mouth twisted into a smirk. "She'll find out soon enough," she said, and trudged back upstairs.

Elly was disappointed that her detective work had yielded what seemed to be a dead end—but was excited by further clues as to what these women actually did.

She filed these away with the many other clues she was now gathering from the women at Crapper Jack's. By now, they had decided that Elly was just "a mite peculiar" and warmed to her, even treated her as a sort of pet. At the end of the night when things were slow, they would gather around the piano, ask for their favorite songs, and "let their hair down." Elly was endlessly fascinated by them and mined their chatter for nuggets of information about what they called "extras." This was when the men paid the bar a dollar to buy the women out before the night was finished and escorted them (from what Elly could gather) to either their homes or a hotel room.

But exactly what occurred then remained a tantalizing mystery.

"How was your extra last night, Dolly?"

"Oh Criminy, plumb wore me out, he did. How bout yours?"

"Well I wish! Them elder gents are all smoochin and no scroochin."

"Ha! That moss-backed ol coot looked dead in the shell, all right…"

All this accompanied by the same knowing looks and ribald laughter Elly had heard from the hoboes around the campfire.

Together with these new clues, Elly was now quite sure that whatever it was they did with the men must be exhausting. Did they wrestle? And was it actually possible that, from other things she was hearing, they did it with their clothes off?

The very idea shocked, confused—and tantalized her.

As she grew comfortable with the job, Elly was once again able to lose herself in the music. Between numbers she would glance at Curly, the moon-faced bouncer, for what sort of dance to play next. From across the bar he would mouth "polka," and she would nod. And a moment later she would be absorbed in the sprightly rhythms and flashing colors of "Hot Time in the Old Town Tonight," and the world would fade from view.

But during her breaks the dancing continued to the music of piano rolls, and she would often lay down her book to study the pageant of forced flirtation and pseudo-courtship swirling all around her. She was surprised to discover it was not the prettiest girls who got the most dances and coveted "extras," but the ones, like mannish Mamie, who smiled, joked with the men, patted their arms, and clung to them when they danced. And she realized it wasn't beauty so much as human warmth and companionship the men were seeking.

These impressions were reinforced by the arrival of a new girl.

It was obvious right away that she was different. There were others, such as cross-eyed Iris, as young—for she couldn't have been more than sixteen or seventeen. Uncommonly pretty, with long auburn hair, a heart-shaped face, and big green eyes—but there were other pretty girls. No, it was her manner. An unlikely mixture of fear—and something very like pride.

Elly began to watch her curiously. Sure enough, despite her beauty, the men who danced with her usually danced but once, for her disinterested gaze and listless manner repelled them as surely as if she had spit in their eye. And any man foolish enough to try and snatch a kiss (granted by most girls at the conclusion of a dance as a matter of course) received looks that, had the girl been a goddess, would surely have turned them to stone.

All this Elly noted with interest. But not nearly as much interest, she quickly realized, as Jimmy.

Elly had been amused to note that the reticence Jimmy had displayed dancing with Martha quickly left him. And since the money they made (split fifty-fifty as always) enabled Jimmy to pay for a hundred dances a night, he was spending quite a lot of each evening on the dance floor, and even began to acquire a certain style. So Jimmy had been one of those to receive a listless dance and stone-faced stare on the girl's first night. And ever since then, Elly noticed, he watched her. Studied her, even. With a look on his face Elly had never seen before.

Jimmy's interest in the girl made Elly watch her even more closely. So both of them noticed the time an old, bearded, unkempt miner approached her with his dance ticket—only to have her shake her head. When it became a habit, Crapper Jack took her aside one night and gave her what must have been an ultimatum. For she nodded like a chastened schoolgirl and danced with anyone after that.

But always with the same remote expression.

So it came as a surprise, the night Elly looked up from her book and saw a man dancing with her a second time. Jimmy noticed as well (though he made a show of disinterest, leaning back and eyeing them from underneath the brim of his derby, looking about as relaxed as a coiled rattlesnake). The man was younger and better-dressed than most, and after the third song they danced in a row, she saw him whisper something in her ear with a look of urgency. Her pale face flushed pink, but she finally nodded. And as Elly began her next set, she saw them walking out of the bar together.

Jimmy proceeded to get drunk. So drunk that when an equally inebriated miner cornered Elly at the end of the last set, forced her to endlessly repeat "Silver Threads Among the Gold" (a treacly tune she detested) and Jimmy got up to rescue her, he stumbled and fell. So she was forced to again play the hateful song, until Curly finally told the man to "stop pestering the little lady or I'll throw ya out on yer ear!"

The next night, Jimmy sat with Elly on her first break, nursing a drink and looking like a person resolving to throw himself under a train, and when Elly next looked up from her book, he was waltzing with the girl. As the piano roll ground out "The Band Played On," they spun around, and she could see Jimmy whispering in her ear and doing his best to charm her. Now and then the girl would favor him with a flashing smile, which Jimmy, flushed with success, would return.

Elly began her next set with another waltz—it was the dance Jimmy did best—and was happy to see them dancing together again. On her next break she looked up to find him steering the girl toward her table.

"Elly, hey Elly—this here's Sara."

"Hello Elly," said Sara, as Jimmy pulled a chair out for her.

Elly said "hello" and set down her book, her usual feelings of dismay trumped this time by curiosity. Sara was saying nice things about her playing. Elly nodded, tried to look into her pretty green eyes, but as usual, couldn't find anything to say in reply but a murmured "thank you."

"Hey now Sara, don't you worry if Elly don't seem like she got much to say for herself," said Jimmy, leaning back and waving his arm expansively. And Elly could see just how nervous he was. "Jus the way she is, she don't mean no offense."

"That's all right," said Sara in a low, musical voice. "Them others here all talk too much."

"Got that right," said Jimmy. "Jus gabble gabble all night long—reg'lar chicken coop." He did a chicken imitation, flapping his elbows. Sara looked both amused and annoyed, and Elly wanted to crawl under the table. She was suddenly determined to prove Jimmy wrong about her muteness and said the kind of thing she had noticed people said when first meeting.

"Have you," she said, "have you been in Cripple Creek long?"

Sara smiled and nodded. "Ever since I can remember. My folks come here from Arkansas when I was three."

"I heard it was a heap wilder back then," said Jimmy.

Sara nodded. "They was lots of prospectors, and lots of sharps tryin to fleece em. So they was some fights when folks got rooked. Least," she added, "that's what my daddy said. I mostly just went to school like a good girl, tried to help mama round the tent—we's livin in a tent for a longish time."

"They had a school?" Elly thought to ask, feeling proud of herself.

"Uh-huh," said Sara. Now that she was more animated, Elly could see how truly pretty she was. "Course it was just a bitty little thing. Not many families in Cripple back then. Just a lot of men. Like here," she concluded, glancing around the room with a wry smile.

"Your daddy a prospector?" asked Jimmy.

Sara's face lost its animation. "Yeah, at first." She began to roll the glass of watered-down whiskey Jimmy had bought her between her open palms. "Then he was a miner, cause he didn't have no luck. Then he died." She lifted the glass and took a long drink, set it down, and began playing with it again. "That was a long time ago. Mama passed away just a few months back. Lungs give out on her."

There was an uncomfortable silence.

"Ol Elly here, her folks is dead too," offered Jimmy.

Elly kicked him under the table.

"That's too bad," said Sara, looking kindly at Elly. "Ain't it tough, though! I guess that's why you're workin here, huh?"

Elly nodded.

"Yeah, well me too." Sara made a face. "Ain't life just the sorrowfullest thing."

"So," said Jimmy by way of changing the subject, "back then, was they gunfights in the street an such?"

Sara's face paled. She closed her eyes and began shaking her head in a confused way. "Yes... No... I don't 'member." Abruptly she pushed back her chair, muttered, "I'm sorry, I gotta go," and—with a stricken look—stood up and rushed away.

But even more stricken was Jimmy. Who drank too much again, and moped all the way home.

"Why'd she run away, Elly? Huh? We's gettin on like a house afire—then she jus run out on me. Why'd she do that to me?"

Elly shook her head for the hundredth time as he leaned against her and they staggered along (though she privately wondered if it was the mention of gunfighting that, for some reason, had scared Sara off).

"Did yer see them eyes a hers, Elly? Give me palpitations ever time I look inside em. But why'd she do it, Elly? Why'd she run out on me like that? An jus when we's gettin on so good..."

•   •   •

Elly awoke and stretched her limbs with a delicious feeling of reprieve. Between her job and her apprenticeships with Lucas and old Sam (with whom she continued to study the art of ragging songs), she had little free time. But today was Sunday, her day off—and, she had decided, her day for adventuring.

The week before, Lucas had made good on his promise to take her fishing. The two of them had set off (with Moosie in tow) bundled up in sweaters, for it was late September and the morning air brisk. Elly had wondered if they would fish in Cripple Creek—there was, after all, a body of water by that name—but Lucas told her it had been poisoned by run-off from the mines. So they hiked over the hills to another stream.

The air was crystalline, and the whole world sparkled. The aspens seemed to have drawn that precious gold everyone was seeking up through the roots and into their rustling leaves. A herd of bighorn sheep in new winter coats appeared at the top of a neighboring hill, gazed at them with regal disdain, then bounded away.

Lucas and Moosie were ideal companions, for Lucas seldom spoke, while Moosie was perfectly happy to do all the work of conversing. Though her remarks were often somewhat obscure, for Moosie apparently felt that sentences—like train passengers—shouldn't be forced to associate just because fate had placed them in close proximity. Thus she might follow the observation that "Eli has shiny boots" with the revelation that she was going to "climb that mountain all the way up, up to the clouds!" Leaving Elly to wonder if there was some tantalizing link she was missing.

They descended into another valley where many of the trees had been reduced to curiously pointed stumps, and found a stream divided into tiered, sky-reflecting pools—like a string of watery blue pearls—by cunningly engineered wooden dams.

"Beavers," said Lucas.

For a long time they caught no fish, for it proved impossible to restrain Moosie from splashing around the edges of the pools they were fishing, throwing sticks in the water, and sending the dark shapes of fish streaking away in all directions. But Lucas was patient, and waited until the wet and exhausted little girl lay passed out on a bed of emerald-colored moss. Then, using grasshoppers he had caught on their hike, he pulled a mess of fat silvery trout from a single pool, as Elly scooped them up in a net.

They returned in time for Hannah to fry them up in cornmeal for the whole boarding house (though it took a while to talk Lucas into staying for dinner, and he spent the entire meal staring at his plate). And when Moosie somehow contrived to fall through the toilet seat in the outhouse, Elly decided the ensuing shrieks, daring rescue, and heroic clean-up made a perfect ending to a day of adventure.

But today she had no special plans. She padded into the kitchen in her robe, poured herself a cup of coffee from the big enamel pot permanently simmering on the stove, and joined Bill and Hannah at the kitchen table. She had already heard them through her bedroom wall arguing about money and mining. Hannah ceased her harangue long enough to say good morning, then returned to these perennial subjects, addressing Elly as though she were a jury to be convinced.

"Elly, what would you say about a man who ran the same mine for four blessed years without even breaking even, actually *losing* money each year? Wouldn't you say"—she began stabbing at Bill's chest with an accusing finger—"wouldn't you agree he must be the most pigheaded," (stab) "stubborn," (stab) "cock-eyed," (stab) "loco roadrunner of a fool that ever swung a pick?"

Bill grinned at Elly during this onslaught. She thrilled to feel his pale blue eyes upon her and tried her best to smile back. It had taken a while to work out that, despite his homespun manner, Bill had a degree in geology. And he was leasing a mine called the Cresson—leasing it for a song because everyone considered it a lost cause—and had a team of miners, including the Englishman Harold Baxter, working for him.

"But one of these days, Hannah," said Bill mildly. "One of these days…"

Elly had heard him say it before and knew it to be a joke between them.

"Oh, *pshaw*," said Hannah. "One of these days I'll play the piano like Elly, and the stove will get up and dance a jig."

Suddenly Elly knew what she wanted today's adventure to be.

"I want," she said to Bill, "I want to see your mine."

~~~

Today was Bill's day off—Harold Baxter, his chief assistant, was overseeing the crew—but he said he would be happy to give Elly a tour. She donned her overalls, and they set off on the interurban, the electric train that connected all the small mining towns in the valley, and the way most miners rode to work. Elly loved riding on it and had already thoroughly explored the route as one of her adventures. On a late Sunday morning, they had the car to themselves. And to sit next to Bill, just the two of them, listening to him talk of gold mining, was maybe even better than waltzing with him.

"Did you know, Elly, that this entire valley"—he waved his arms at the distant hills—"is actually the crater of an extinct volcano?"

Elly was amazed. She shook her head.

"A huge one—four miles across. They call them calderas, craters this big. And that's the whole reason for what's going on here. See, that volcano just blew off the granite crust that covers most of the Rockies and exposed the minerals underneath. There's at least a little gold in all the land around us, and rich veins criss-crossing the whole valley."

"But," said Elly, marveling at this (and at Bill's unusual loquaciousness), "but your mine doesn't have one?"

"A rich vein? Haven't found one yet. But here's the thing: the Cresson's surrounded by mines full of high-grade ore. And the folks that first mined it didn't do a very systematic job. Which is what I'm trying to do. And, well…"

"One of these days?" suggested Elly.

"That's right," said Bill, grinning. "One of these days."

~~~

They got off the train at the base of a huge hill riddled with mine shafts. Monstrous piles of loose rock, evidence of the colossal extent to which man had perforated the interior of the hill, were shored up against its sides. Precarious looking wooden structures extended the tracks leading from the mine shafts out into the open air, like train bridges leading to nowhere. They watched a cart full of ore emerge from a distant shaft pushed by two antlike men. They tipped it sideways down a chute into a train car below. Only after the dust began to settle did the sound reach them.

"Is that the Cresson?" asked Elly.

Bill shook his head and pointed to another shaft closer to them where nothing was happening. They climbed a switch-back trail, just wide enough for a mule wagon, blasted from the rocky, treeless slope. Twenty minutes later they came to a wooden shack near the top. Black smoke poured from a pipe jutting from the roof. Piles of lumber, coal, old packing crates, and broken machinery littered the bleak windswept landscape.

A man emerged from the shack and, holding his hat to his head against the wind, hurried toward them.

"Mister Vin," he said. He made a motion to touch the brim of his hat before clamping it to his head again. "I didn't tink—"

"George," said Bill, "I'm going to show this young lady here around. We got a helmet that'll fit her?"

"Sure sure, no problem Mister Vin."

They followed him into the shack. The air inside was hot and damp. In the center of the shack was a yawning black hole. An idling steam engine—perhaps, thought Elly, one of the ones she'd watch Lucas disassemble—took up most of the rest of the space. George pushed a lever, there was a loud CLUNK, and a winch mounted over the hole began pulling something up to the surface on a cable. Rummaging in a corner, George produced two helmets with brass lamps mounted on their brims. He unscrewed the tops of the lamps, poured something from a kettle inside them, resealed them, and handed them to Bill.

"Dat one, Mister Vin. Oughta fit her."

She thrilled to the gentle touch of Bill's strong hands as he adjusted her chinstrap. He put on his own helmet, flicked something at the top that ignited his lamp, then did the same to hers.

A large, open elevator car was rising from the ground. George threw a lever, and it stopped abruptly.

"Well Elly, you ready?"

Suddenly Elly found herself having second thoughts. But she nodded.

"Everybody down on the twelfth level, George?"

"Ya, cept Yannie an Bela, they's on the eighth shorin up loose pilings. Had a blast bout, oh, couple hours ago. Maybe nudder one soon."

Bill helped Elly step onto the lift and, still holding her arm, nodded at George. He pushed a lever—and with a jerk they began to descend.

The square of dim light above them began to grow smaller, and soon it was totally dark but for the faint illumination from their lamps. Elly was reminded of Alice falling down the rabbit hole. They passed a dark tunnel heading off to one side.

"His name's really Gyorgy—something like that—but I call him George. I do that with a lot of these foreign follows. Just can't bring myself to call a man Luigi, know what I mean? So I just say 'Louie.'"

Elly sensed Bill was saying these things to calm her and was glad of it (and of his hand still gently resting on her shoulder) for the tunnels, which continued to drift by at regular intervals, disappeared into bleak depths their lamps did nothing to penetrate, and filled her with dread. She looked up at him—then immediately wished she hadn't, for the way her lamp lit the underside of his face made him look ghastly. He rang a bell mounted on the side of the lift, and they jerked to a stop.

"Twelfth level," said Bill, helping her step across the gaping crack between the lift and the tunnel.

From all around echoed the sounds of brute labor. Elly couldn't help but compare these "levels" to the various numbered circles of Hell in Dante's *Inferno* that Professor Carp had mentioned. The impression was reinforced when they set off down the tunnel and encountered beings with lights shining from their foreheads like one-eyed demons, who ceased their shoveling and drilling to murmur greetings to Bill in queer accents, as if he were Satan himself.

They followed a set of narrow train tracks. Up ahead, a string of small, metal ore cars was dimly visible. Suddenly there was a yell followed by a thundering sound, and the cars disappeared in a cataclysm of falling rock and dust. Elly felt herself scream, but the sound was lost in the tumult. When the dust settled, she saw that one of the cars was full of rock.

"See?" Bill was saying, unaware of the turmoil in her mind. "That's how we get the ore from one level to another." They reached the car and Bill pointed to a chute in the tunnel's ceiling. He called a greeting to someone above them, and began explaining something about ventilation. But Elly could hardly take in the words. Or think at all.

The nightmare feeling she had been fighting now took possession of her. As in a dream, she let Bill guide her to the end of the tunnel. There she was introduced to another one-eyed demon who claimed to be Harold Baxter ("Come to see a bit of minin, 'ave we?") and a squat, trollish figure wearing a vest bristling with coils of wire and obscure tools, that Bill referred to as the "Powder Monkey." Indeed, he was scuttling about in a most apelike way, tapping cylinders into deep holes drilled in the rock, then stringing wires connecting them all. Somewhere bells began ringing, and they all jogged quickly back up the tunnel. More alarms were going off, a terrible clangor, everyone was crouching down, and Bill pulled Elly down beside him—

There was a sound so loud that everything went silent. The earth shook and trembled beneath her—just as it had so long ago, and in the terrible dreams she'd had ever since. And once again something in Elly's mind gave way...

She woke up with the sun in her eyes.

"Oh Elly, oh dear Lord, Elly—"

"She's comin round, Gov'ner!"

Bill's face was close to hers. Above him a circle of heads, silhouetted by the sun, stared down at her. She blinked, dazzled.

"Elly," said Bill again, stroking her face. "Elly, tell me you're all right?"

She managed to nod.

"Oh thank the good Lord," said Bill—and he kissed her forehead.

~~~

Later she she would decide it had all been worth it.

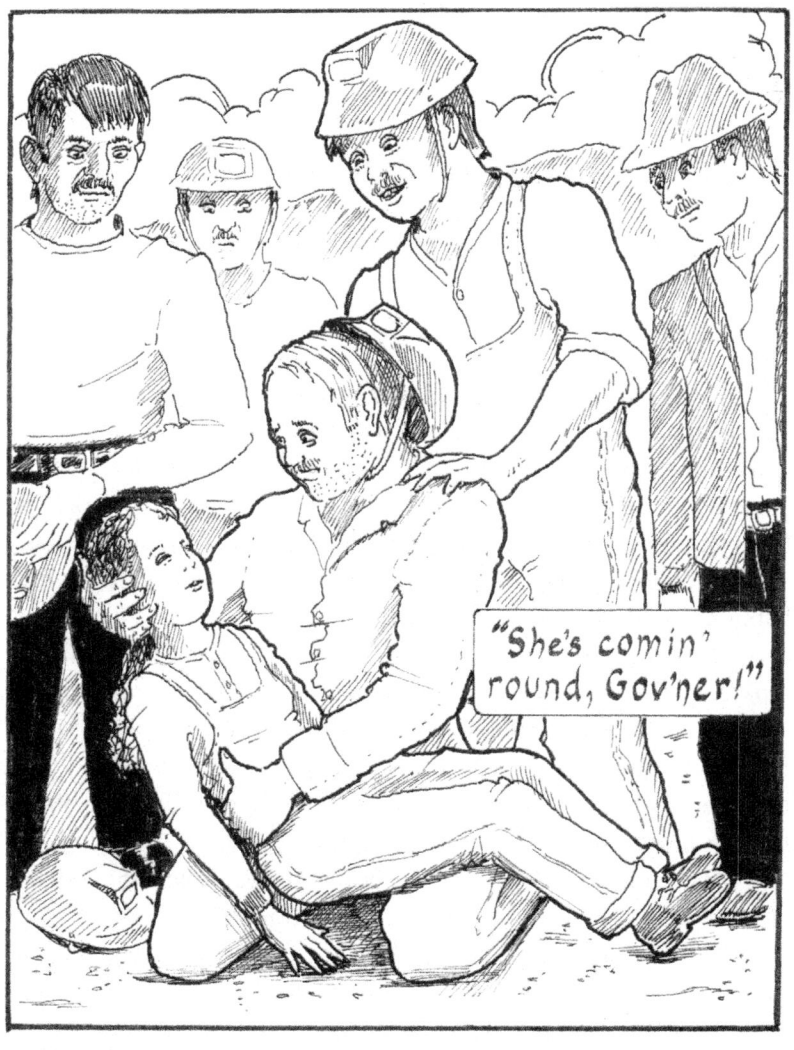

Chapter Five

An Invitation

Jimmy was persistent, and it wasn't many days before Elly spied him dancing with Sara again. He wore a new suit of blue serge with thin yellow striping, his hair was carefully trimmed, oiled, and parted down the middle, and Elly was struck by how handsome he had become. Sara smiled and gazed into his good eye and allowed him to hold her closer than she'd let anyone else. And Elly felt Jimmy's happiness as though it were her own.

But when she played the last chords of "After the Ball" and looked for them again, everything seemed to have gone wrong. Jimmy was squeezing Sara's hand and seemed to be begging her for something. Sara had turned away from him with her eyes squeezed shut, her face twisted as though in pain, shaking her head. Until Jimmy finally stalked away with a black expression.

This time when they walked home, he was cold sober, kicked viciously at loose stones, and never said a word.

The next night he flirted with some of the other girls. But Elly saw plainly it was all for show, and the show was directed at Sara. Who gave him glances at first quietly beseeching, then—as the night went on and Jimmy continued to ignore her—becoming more and more irritated.

Finally, she walked up to where Elly and Jimmy were sitting together during her last break and sat down without invitation.

"Look," she said to Jimmy. "You want to come home with me so durn bad, well come on then."

Jimmy stared at her.

"But only," she added, glancing at Elly, "only if she comes too."

Jimmy's mouth fell open. "But that," he finally sputtered, "that don't make no damn—"

"That's the deal," said Sara. She began to rise.

Jimmy swallowed. "Yeah, okay," he said.

He paid his dollar to buy her out, and a few minutes later the three of them were picking their way through the grim lanes of Poverty Gulch, the aptly-named part of Cripple Creek where the poorest miners lived in rickety shacks and tents. A cold wind whipped down the dark, stinking lane, and Elly stepped in a fresh pile of horse manure. Sara marched along as though they weren't even there. No one said a word.

Finally, Sara turned off the rutted track and leapt over a foul-smelling ditch. They followed her, and she led them inside a dark cave of a hut smelling of coal smoke and the ghosts of greasy meals past. She lit an oil lamp, and they found themselves in a single windowless room with a coal stove, a bed, a small table and two chairs, a sideboard littered with pots and dishes, and not much else. On the bed, beneath a pile of old quilts, lay the shape of a small sleeping figure.

The room was cold. Sara set the lamp on the table, opened the stove, and threw a few lumps of coal on the embers. More acrid smoke filled the room, making Elly's eyes smart.

"Durn thing leaks," said Sara. She kicked the stove shut with a clang. The figure beneath the quilts stirred. Brown curls peeped out from the edges of the blanket. She saw Jimmy staring.

"That's Jonah," she said.

Jimmy looked a question at her.

"My brother."

Jimmy nodded. "How old is he?"

"Just turned eight."

Elly was looking at an old tin-type hanging above the sideboard. A man in an old-fashioned suit stood stiffly beside a seated woman in a white dress. Both were very young and wore pale-eyed, startled expressions as though facing a firing squad.

"That's my daddy and mama," said Sara. "On their weddin day. Bout all I got left of em."

Jimmy examined it. "She's pretty," he declared. "Like you."

Sara said nothing to this. She waved them to the two chairs and sat on the edge of the bed. The room was so small they faced each other across the table. The light from the oil lamp gave all their faces a sickly yellowish pallor. Sara looked at Jimmy.

"I ain't never brought no man back here, and I never will." She reached over and gently lay her hand atop her brother's sleeping form and made the reason plain. "Don't know why I brought you."

She sat up again and hugged herself. Stared at her feet. Took a deep breath.

"Just seems like you're so hell-bent on gettin to know me. Well, look around." She waved a hand at their grim surroundings. "This is my life. Pretty, huh?"

She stared defiantly at Jimmy. He blinked at her, twisting his derby in his hand.

"Ain't no shame in bein poor," he finally said. "Me an Elly, we was up against it for the longest time. Slept on the ground, had to beg for handouts. Didn't we, Elly?"

Elly tried to nod, but Sara had buried her face in her hands and was shaking her head and didn't see her. "Oh, you just don't understand a bit," she said in a muffled voice. She pulled her hands away, and her green eyes flashed at him. "We had a good life! Even when we's livin in a tent, we had nice things. Mama had a rosewood chest, brought it all the way from Arkansas in a wagon. And Daddy bought her a sewin machine, top of the line. She sewed such pretty things with it…" Her eyes were staring beyond Jimmy, into the past. "And

Daddy worked so hard. We got us a nice house, we always had good food. And then...then he went and got hisself killed."

Sara's face had gone hard. Jimmy stared at her, then reached past the lamp and squeezed her hand. "But it ain't your fault," he said. "Ain't your fault he got hisself killed and now yez up against it."

Sara seemed to crumple. She snatched her hand from his and buried her face in her hands again. "But that's just it—it *is*! It *is* my fault, it's all my fault..."

Jimmy gaped at her in confusion. Sara shook her head back and forth. Suddenly she looked up and began to speak in a rush, in a pleading voice rising and falling with emotion.

"But, but—how was I s'posed to know? I was just a kid, not much older than Jonah is now, how was I s'posed to know that the things I heard em talking bout would lead to folks gettin killed? It was just this feller I knew—we all knew him, us kids, cept I must of figgered what I heard him talkin bout with this other feller sounded important, so I told Daddy. Oh!" she exclaimed suddenly, pounding the bedclothes with her fists. "Why I'm even *talkin* to you bout all this stuff? Y'all don't know *nothin* bout that time!"

Elly cleared her throat. "Was it," she ventured, "was it about the union?"

Sara nodded mournfully. "Wasn't it just? Wasn't everything about the blame union back then? It was 'Federation this' and 'Federation that'! I got so sick of hearin Daddy talk about it..."

She closed her eyes and bit her lip, took a deep breath, and plunged on.

"But I was just a little fool, and I thought Daddy would want to know bout the things I heard those fellers talkin bout. And Daddy must've went and told someone else cause they come in the middle of the night, two men with neckerchiefs coverin their faces, and they pulled Daddy out of bed and Jonah's screamin, him just a little tiny baby. And one of em says it's too bad about those things Daddy heard. And they both have guns, and one of em's got his gun pointed at me and Mama, and Daddy says, 'For God's sake, don't hurt em.' And that's the last words he ever spoke cause the other one shot him in the head. Just blew his brains out right there in front of us, then shot him twicet more while he's lyin on the ground to make sure. And it wasn't him—it was *me* that heard em! It was all cause of *me*!"

She pounded the bed again, her pretty face twisted in anguish. Jonah stirred and made a whimpering sound. She bent down and murmured something in his ear and stroked his hair, and he quieted. As she pulled the blankets back up Elly caught a glimpse of an elfin little face.

"He's about the only thing I got left, you know? Just me and him now." She stroked Jonah's sleeping form. "You got any idea what I'm talkin about?"

Jimmy gave a slight nod.

"So anyways, after Mama died last year, I had to sell stuff so's we could live. She was sewin to support us, but the last six months she got to coughin so bad she could hardly sew at all. I tried to do some, but I just don't have the knack. We had to move here. She died in this bed. After she passed, I sold her sewin machine. Sold her rosewood chest, all her pretty clothes. Sold her weddin ring to buy coal, or last winter we would of froze. Even sold her weddin gown—she said it was for me to keep and get married in but I *had* to sell it. And now, well, seems like I only got one thing left to sell."

She fixed Jimmy with a look. He swallowed. She turned and put her hand again on Jonah.

"And," she said in a soft, determined voice, "I don't care. Cause I will do *whatever it takes*—you hear me? Just whatever it takes so's he can have good food and clothes and a warm house and maybe someday we can get the hell out of this place."

Again she stared at Jimmy defiantly. He stared right back at her. They sat that way, all three of them, for a long time. No one said a word.

Finally Elly spoke.

"That man you knew. The one you heard talking. What was his name?"

Sara made a disgusted sound. "What's it matter now? All that's in the past." But when Elly continued to stare at her (in a way she never did), Sara finally rolled her eyes and said: "Harry Orchard. His name was Harry Orchard."

She rose from the bed and stood in front of the stove with her back to them, hugging herself.

"You best go," she said.

The walk home that night was an icy and silent affair, and next morning Elly's tiny room was so cold she could scarcely make herself get out of bed. She kicked her door open, then lay a while longer, letting the faint heat coming from the kitchen stove seep into the room. But when she finally got hurriedly dressed, she could still see her breath.

It was only mid-October, but a thin layer of snow had fallen. A fickle wind blew the dry, powdery flakes around like someone carelessly dusting. Inside the cavernous machine shop it was almost as cold. She found Lucas next to the stove reassembling a gear box. He neither spoke nor looked at her, but she knew he knew she was there. She sat down next to him and began handing him parts in the order she had memorized when she watched him take it apart, putting small assemblies together to save him time.

They had worked companionably without a word for an hour (both Elly and her tools gradually losing their chill), when Mr. Smithson called for Lucas to "come outside for a minute." They found him in conversation with a man standing next to an automobile hitched to a team of horses. This confused Elly, until she noticed the front end was smashed on one side. It was a jaunty little thing with a dark blue body and black fenders. On a shiny brass radiator, the word "Ford" was written in flowing script.

"Model T Roadster," murmured Lucas reverently, before crawling underneath the vehicle.

"...and well," the man was saying, "I don't know, but I reckon the good Lord just didn't intend for me to own a motorcar. Maybe His way of tellin me I'm makin too much money."

"Could be He's tellin you you're lucky you ain't dead," remarked Smithson genially. "Run off the road, did ya?"

"Well," said the man, "that wasn't the sensation." He had a sleek brown beard and wore a fur hat and expensive-looking, full-length fur coat so that he was more or less continuous. "No, it felt more like the road got bored with my company and struck out for somewheres else, then tossed a tree in my path out of spite."

Lucas emerged from underneath the vehicle and began to vigorously yank on the crumpled housing covering one side of the engine. It opened with a bang. He and Elly peered inside.

"What say, Lucas?" said Smithson. Lucas continued his inspection as though he hadn't heard. Mr. Smithson waited patiently.

"Bent frame and front axle," he said finally.

"What about the engine?"

Lucas made no answer. He climbed into the drivers seat, fiddled with some levers, then jumped out and tried to roll the vehicle. But it wouldn't budge. He walked to the rear and examined the tracks in the snow.

"Were the rear wheels locked when you pulled it?" he murmured, not looking at anyone.

"Well now," said the man, stroking his beard reflectively, "it did seem a mite contrary to being drug."

"Drive train's frozen," said Lucas.

"Can you fix it?" asked Smithson.

Lucas stood still, considering. "Need parts," he said.

"Tell you what," said the man, "just do what it takes, then sell it for me. Paid almost seven hundred for it. But hell, my mine's makin almost that a ton these days. Just get whatever you can for the infernal thing."

Lucas helped him unhitch the horses from the vehicle. One of them had been saddled in advance, and the man galloped away as if in a hurry to put his automobiling behind him. Together Lucas and Smithson got the back wheels up on dollies, and they rolled it into the shop.

"Just give me a list of what it needs, and I'll send it off to Detroit," said Smithson, ambling off to his office.

Lucas stood contemplating the engine with a rapt expression. "Four cylinder. Solid block. First engine in the world with a detachable head," he murmured. He peered at Elly with his funny half-smile.

"This is gonna be fun."

~~~

The two of them spent the rest of the day starting to disassemble the Ford. As with everything she did, Elly was completely concentrated on their work. So it wasn't until she began walking home that she thought again about the events of the previous evening. The sun had come out, and its intense glare had melted all but a few shaded patches of snow and turned the road to mud. As she stepped to avoid the puddles, she ran through Sara's terrible story in her mind, marveling how it fit together with all the other clues she had been gathering. She recalled the stubborn assertion of the man at the Fourth of July dance that "there was a witness." And over and over, in the conversations she had overheard, the same name. Whispered under people's breath or murmured reluctantly. A name which made people eager to change the subject.

She was determined to get to the bottom of it all.

"Who is Harry Orchard?"

Elly was used to people looking surprised whenever she said anything unsolicited. But this time, the faces around the dining room table looked almost comically stupefied.

"Oh Lord, Elly," said Hannah, breaking the silence. "Whatever made you bring that man's name up?"

Bill cleared his throat. "He was a miner, Elly. And he did some terrible, misguided things in the name of the union."

"And you knew him, right Bill?" said Eli eagerly. Elly remembered he'd asked the same thing once before.

"Hell, we *all* knew him," said Pinky, disgusted. "Used to spout off at the Federation meetings so much that folks thought he must be a paid agitator. But no one took him serious. Thought he was just another high-grader who happened to be a hot-head."

"What's a high-grader?" asked Elly. Being a detective seemed to loosen her tongue.

"A high-grader's a bloke sneaks high-grade ore out of the mine to sell it for 'imself,'" said Harold Baxter.

"Yeah, old Harry had a sweet set-up too," said Pinky. "Most fellers just hide it in their lunch pails, or their clothing. But Harry found a back way out of the Vindicator and was taking it out wholesale, by the wheelbarrow load. But he was such a gentle-like fellow, mostly. Played ball with the kids when he got off his shift. Kept his cabin neat as a woman. No one would've ever thought he'd do somethin that crazy."

"Well darn it all, what did he do?" asked Jimmy. Zachary Crabbe raised his pimply face from his plate, and Elly realized they were both as curious as she was.

"Well," said Pinky, "he—"

"He killed my Daddy!" cried Martha, who had been in and out of the kitchen during their conversation, clearing away the dinner. She flung the dessert on the table and ran back into the kitchen in tears. Hannah cast a reproving glance at Elly, then started after her.

Elly would have crawled under the table, but that would have drawn even more attention to herself. An argument started up between Harold Baxter and Nils, the Norwegian miner, over who would be the first to the South Pole, Scott or Amundsen, each rooting for his own countryman. But that conversational vein had long been played out and seemed a patent attempt to change the subject.

The result, yet again, of mentioning that fateful name.

Yet even in her mortification, Elly could not stop her mind from processing these new clues and trying to fit them into the puzzle. For Hannah had once told her Martha's father had been a "scab miner" (she really must find out what that word "scab" meant), killed in a depot explosion. And now she knew who had caused that explosion: Harry Orchard.

Old Sam had told Elly the first snowfall was a signal to him to "make like a goose and head south for the winter," so that week she had her last lesson in ragging songs. She was playing a ragged-up version of "Give My Regards to Broadway," rocking out the left hand chords in the strong, steady way she had learned and embellishing the melody with the arsenal of licks she had picked up from her mentor. Chorus after chorus she played, solving creative problems on the fly, like an acrobat performing death-defying leaps without a net—when she suddenly felt herself being rudely shoved aside. Old Sam grinned at her and jumped on the song without missing a beat, and Elly realized he was trying to "cut" her. She let him play a couple of choruses then pushed him aside and, with childish glee, jumped in his place and played another wildly inspired chorus. Sam chuckled. And shoved her off the bench again…

A few minutes later Elly, who never laughed, was leaning against Sam unable to catch her breath from laughter, while Sam sat next to her with his arm around her waist, muttering, "Oh dear Lord, sweet Jesus," with tears in his eyes.

"Well Miss Elly," he finally said, letting go of her to wipe his face with his handkerchief, "I declare, ain't got nothin left to teach you. Yessir, you done squeezed old Sam dry." He pulled off his derby and mopped his bald spot. Still chuckling, he looked at her with mischievous eyes. "You know, you play that a-way, people gone think you got colored blood."

Elly knew she had gotten the highest compliment.

Now that Sara had unburdened herself, Elly had hoped she and Jimmy would finally come together, and was happy to see them step out onto the dance floor again. But when, at the dance's conclusion, Jimmy had whispered something in Sara's ear, she had again reacted by shaking her head stubbornly and twisting away from him. Jimmy tried dancing with her a few more times, but she no longer leaned against him, and her easy smile had been replaced by a polite mask; it was as though they had become strangers.

Then Jimmy must have finally given up on her, for he left her alone. But Elly would catch him watching her from afar with a look that was hurt, perplexed, and disgusted in equal measure. While the expression on his face, when she allowed the occasional man to buy her out, made Elly ache for him.

One cold gray afternoon Elly decided to neglect Lucas in favor of detective work.

She rode the interurban to Victor, the valley's second-largest town. The main street was very short, and she easily found the small brick building where the *Victor and Cripple Creek Express* was published. Inside it seemed even smaller, with desks and machinery all crammed into one room, and the rhythmic clank of the presses jarred her brain so she could hardly think.

A harried-looking man wearing a green eyeshade looked up from a desk piled with papers and blinked at her.

"Yes?"

Clank... Clank... Clank... Elly stared stupidly at him.

"Are you dumb?"

She made an effort to collect herself, and managed to stutter that she wanted to look at back issues.

"How far back?" said the man, tapping his pencil impatiently.

"Back to the time of Harry Orchard."

She was not surprised when the name provoked a reaction. This time it was emphatic head-shaking.

"No no no. Back then this was a union paper, and all the back issues were destroyed by the militia. They tried to wipe the Federation off the map, don't you know? And they pretty much succeeded, because now we're just an ordinary newspaper."

He returned to the manuscript he was editing, and Elly realized she had been dismissed. At a nearby desk a young man wearing rimless spectacles gave her a sympathetic glance. A minute later she was standing outside the building and feeling rather discouraged, when she realized someone was standing next to her.

The bespectacled young man pulled a cigarette from a gold case and lit it.

"Hey look—I couldn't help but overhear. You really need to know about that awful time?"

Elly nodded hopefully.

"Huh," he said. He took a long drag on his cigarette, staring thoughtfully into the distance, then exhaled. "Right, well… You need to talk to Emma. Emma Langdon. She helped put out the Federation paper back then. Fought the militia when they tried to shut it down. Made her famous for a spell; they called her the 'Joan of Arc of Cripple Creek.'"

He chuckled and took another drag on his cigarette. "She and her husband were both radicals, all tied up with the union. She can tell you everything about what happened back then. Her husband's one of the fellows got himself banished from the state, but she stayed on. One of the last union hold-outs, won't give up the fight, so she's not too popular right now. Keeps to herself. Lives on Portland Street, three blocks down, that direction…"

~~~

Five minutes later she stood in front of a plain brown cottage, its white trim stained grayish-yellow by hard winters. A tiny woman, a head shorter than Elly, opened the door. She was perhaps in her late thirties, with auburn hair piled carelessly atop her head and held in place with a tortoise shell comb. Her mouth and nose were as small and neat as her person, and her face dominated by a pair of intelligent brown eyes. Which now peered inquiringly up at Elly.

"Yes? What is it you want?" She sounded both curious and impatient.

Elly had learned from experience not to mention Harry Orchard right away. "I...I want to know about the union."

The woman's eyes flashed. "Why?"

Elly decided her only chance was to tell the truth. She looked down, composing her words.

"Because I know something that might be important."

The woman looked at her doubtfully. "But...but you must have been a mere child. In fact, you're still a mere child—so you must have been an even *merer* child." She smiled crookedly.

Elly was starting to like her. Again she composed an answer.

"It's someone I met," she paused. "She was a mere child also." Another pause. "But she overheard something."

"Yes? And just what could a young girl have overheard back then that could be so important?" asked Emma (for Elly was sure it must be she) with the same hint of a smile.

"A man talking with Harry Orchard."

Emma's Langdon's eyes widened, and her smile disappeared. But for once the name had a positive effect, for it seemed to be the "Open Sesame" that let Elly into the house. A few minutes later they were facing each other in a small parlor with cups of freshly-brewed tea balanced on their laps. A monstrous stuffed bird stood on a side table, regarding Elly with beady glass eyes.

"Golden eagle," said Emma. She leaned toward Elly, her eyes similarly fixed and intent. "So. What is it your friend overheard?"

"I'm...I'm not exactly sure. But whatever it was, she told her father. And someone had him killed because of it."

Emma Langdon stared hard at Elly, then nodded slowly. "Was her father a Federation man?"

Elly stared at her feet. "I'm pretty sure he was. She wasn't completely clear about it." She thought about what else to say. Emma waited patiently. "But first," said Elly finally, "can you tell me everything about what happened?"

"You're saying you really don't know that much yourself?"

Elly nodded.

"Gosh darn, Elly,"—they had exchanged names but not much else before Emma disappeared to brew the tea—"we could be here a month and a day and I'd still be talking. I mean, I'm even now writing an entire book about the whole thing!" She laughed for the first time, a sudden merry sound that ceased just as abruptly. "But—well, I suppose I could sketch it all in big strokes for you…"

She sat a moment, seeming to compose her thoughts.

"So. What do you know about unions?"

"Very little," admitted Elly.

Emma gave a slightly exasperated sigh. "Well, that's really the most important thing of all to understand. You see, unions are the working man's only weapon against being exploited by the rich. There are unions for all sorts of different trades, more and more every year. And even now, many of them are joining together into a single, powerful union called the— Oh!" She put down her teacup and slapped her own cheek. "I'm already getting so far ahead of myself!"

She shook her head, then continued: "So! In 1893, the Western Federation of Miners was established. Because miners are among the most exploited workers of all. Even though—well, one might think that with vast fortunes being made, the mine owners would be able to pay their workers a decent wage. I mean especially when one considers the long hours they work in dangerous and degrading conditions. If only out of—well, human decency. But"—she shook her head ruefully—"human beings seem not to be constituted this way. Instead, the mine owners pay as little as possible, a pittance in most cases, just to increase their own profits. I'm talking about the basic principles of capitalism here, Elly—do you understand?"

Elly nodded.

Emma studied her speculatively, then continued.

"So! You must understand as well that the union was everything to the miners in this valley. It wasn't just a way to band together and strike for higher wages, better conditions—you do know about strikes?"

Again Elly nodded.

"So it wasn't just for striking. We—the Federation—took care of its members. The union had its own medical clinics, libraries, reading rooms. Organized activities, lectures, self-improvement programs. Even had its own grocery so the miners and their families wouldn't be gouged by the local merchants. And," she concluded, "the Federation had its own newspaper. That was me," she said, flashing her crooked grin, "and my husband Charles.

"So anyway, the mine owners hated the Federation and organized something called 'Citizens United.' A front group of stooges, dupes, and lackeys—well, I'm sorry," she added with schoolmarmish primness, "that's what they were—claiming to represent 'the people.'"

She made a face, sipped her tea, then continued: "Well, in aught three, when the smelter workers in Colorado City struck—you do know what smelters are?"

Elly had to shake her head.

"Ah! That's where all the ore you see being shipped out every day is processed. The workers were making $1.80 a day, working twelve-hour days, even though the Colorado senate had already passed a bill making eight-hour days universal. But the mine owners and other capitalists bribed the state supreme court to strike it down. THAT'S how capitalism works, you see Elly? There is no real democracy, because the rich control everything. It's all a sham!"

Emma's eyes were blazing with fanatical intensity, and Elly felt herself being swept away by the power of the little woman's conviction. She nodded with enthusiasm.

Emma nodded back, satisfied. "But you see, the workers have to stick together; that is their strength. So when the smelter workers struck, the Federation voted to strike as well in support of their cause."

Emma paused. She sipped tea and seemed to gather her forces. "All right. Now I must condense eighteen months of dramatic events. It was a long, terrible strike. The mine owners brought in scab miners—that's non-union workers—"

Elly made a mental note that her question had been answered.

"—then they did even worse things. Planted Pinkerton detectives at the Federation meetings—" She broke off at the sight of Elly's confusion. "The Pinkertons are a sort of private police force—in this case, spies for hire. Worse yet, some were paid to be agitators. The idea was to incite the Federation to violence so there would be a pretext to bring in government forces to suppress the union. And—ultimately—to wipe it out."

She paused dramatically, then continued:

"But the Federation refused to take the agitators' bait, and the strike continued in a peaceful, law-abiding manner. So Governor Peabody (mine owners had him in their pocket, well isn't THAT a surprise!)"—she smiled sardonically—"Peabody decided he didn't need a pretext and sent the militia to Cripple Creek. Led by a man named Sherman Bell. One of Teddy's Rough Riders, don't you know—real 'by jingo' type." Emma rolled her eyes. "Well he took charge, all right. Stationed a thousand dunderheads with loaded rifles all over the valley. They called it the 'National Guard,' isn't that a hoot? As if it were the *nation* it was guarding, and not the vested interests of the mine owners. Constructed a 'bull-pen'—a sort of open-air prison—and locked all the union leaders up. No charges, no trial. Suspended *habeas corpus*. No right to assemble, bear arms—the audacity of the man! Used to charge around on a white horse, sword, feathered hat, as though he were the Emperor of Cripple Creek!"

Emma let loose another merry peal of laughter, then slapped her cheek. "Oh! We'll be here all day, Elly, if I keep on like this." She caught her breath. "So! It wasn't just the Federation leaders who got locked up, but anyone who spoke out in favor of the union. So when our paper dared to criticize the troops in our midst, Sherman Bell figured he'd better muzzle us and double quick. Sent forty-five of his armed hooligans to the newspaper office one night. Locked up the whole staff, including my husband. Well, not quite the whole staff." Emma grinned mischievously. "For what they didn't know was, I'm a trained linotype operator too. So when I got wind of what had happened, I ran down to the office—still in my nightgown!—barricaded myself inside, and got the paper out all by myself."

She pointed to something framed on the wall behind the stuffed eagle. Elly got up to examine it (giving the bird a wide berth) and saw it was the front page of the *Victor Record* from September 30th, 1903. With the big black headline: SOMEWHAT DISFIGURED, BUT STILL IN THE RING!

"I delivered the paper myself the next morning to the men in the bull pen," crowed Emma. "With the ink still wet!"

Elly sat down again, full of admiration for the feisty little woman.

"So! Meanwhile, the mine owners' spies continued agitating at the union meetings, knowing all it would take is one hothead. Someone soft-in-the-head as well. And that person was: Harry Orchard."

Now it was Elly's turn to thrill at the sound of Orchard's name.

"The devil's fool, if ever there was one. A month after they attacked the paper, he set off an explosion at the Vindicator, where he had worked before the strike. They say he knew a back way inside. Meant to kill a bunch of scab miners—but put the bomb on the wrong level and killed two bosses instead. Did I mention he was a fool?

"January of aught four, he tried again. Cut the cable on a lift and sent fifteen miners plunging to their deaths. But some said the cable must have been old and frayed, and nobody knew who to blame. So in June, Harry decided to try again. Took a load of dynamite to the Independence Depot—"

Elly waited, breathless.

"—and set it off at the platform right when the train came in. Killed thirteen scab miners getting off their shift—they say it rained legs with boots still on them—and crippled six more men for life.

"Well! Everyone blamed the Federation for the acts of one fool, and that was the spark that started the riot. With a little help from the mine owners, because it was mobs organized by Citizens United that tore through the streets of Victor and Cripple Creek and destroyed everything related to the union. Two hundred men were banished from the state, deported to Kansas and New Mexico—just dropped off in the middle of nowhere across the state lines. One of them"—Emma's eyes burned into Elly's—"one of them was my husband. And the union—the union was finished."

But Emma looked anything but finished as she continued on: "Oh but Elly, the tide of history is on our side! Charles is still in New Mexico and sends me money to continue the fight here. And only a year after all this happened, I was one of the delegates in Chicago, where a new union was formed—the one I mentioned before—to represent all working men and women everywhere. The I.W.W.—International Workers of the World!"

Emma's face was alight. Perched on the edge of her chair, empty teacup in her hand, the tiny woman seemed to embody some concentrated, indomitable power.

Elly was still trying to assimilate it all. "So," she said, "did they catch Harry Orchard?"

"Now that," said Emma, "is a strange story. A very strange story. No, Harry got away. Ran to Idaho—where he assassinated the ex-governor. Which makes him sound less like a hot-head and more like a saboteur-for-hire, wouldn't you say, hmm?" Emma arched an eyebrow. "Got caught this time. And while he was confessing, decided to confess to all the things he did here as well. Well, now why would he want to do that?" asked Emma rhetorically. "Perhaps—rumor has it—because he was promised a life sentence if he implicated the Federation. A life sentence, instead of the hangman's rope he deserved. And he's still in prison today."

Emma stared at Elly, waiting, and she knew it was her turn.

"My friend overheard someone talking to Harry Orchard."

"Who did she hear? And what were they saying?"

Elly shook her head, wishing she knew more.

"Whatever it was, she told her father. And he must have told someone else. Because two men came to their house in the middle of the night—men with neckerchiefs over their faces—and shot him in cold blood, in front of his entire family."

"Oh, the scoundrels!" exclaimed Emma. "And it *is* interesting—oh, I'm sorry, that's a terrible word to use—tragic, of course that's what it is. But it must mean something. If you find out anything more, will you please let me know?"

Elly nodded eagerly.

"Because you know, here's another interesting thing. Even though Harry Orchard confessed to killing all those people, no one was never prosecuted for any of the crimes he committed here. And if anyone could ever prove who it was pulling his strings…"

She stared hard at Elly, so hard Elly had to look away—only to find herself looking instead into the fierce, unblinking gaze of a golden eagle.

Chapter Six

The Man with the Purple Neck

Jimmy had never felt like this and hoped to Christ he never would again.

To lie in bed with your pimply roommate snoring and farting beside you and make long, mush-brained speeches to the ceiling. To whisper a name, just to hear the sound of it. To have the sight of a girl make your heart swell up inside your chest until it squeezed the breath right out of you. Then to watch her leave the saloon on the arm of some jug-eared piker (looking like he just won the Kentucky Derby) but say no to *him*—the one that can't sleep for dreaming about her!

The brass of the girl! The sheer brass...

But then he would remember going to her home. The things she told him, things he was sure she'd never told any of those others. About how her folks died, about her little brother... Why'd she tell him all that if she didn't care for him? Those words she had said to him, the last time he tried to buy her out, before he gave up. Shaking her head with her face all twisted like he'd asked her to cut off her nose. "I thought you was different," she said.

He puzzled and puzzled on it. Different? Of course he was different! Only one in this whole goddamn town who cared about her, couldn't she see that? The way she looked at him now, like he was some stranger... It just froze his bones.

Then one morning he awoke, and somehow the world felt different. Crabbe, his roommate, was long gone to work, and he lay in bed for a while staring at the ceiling, trying to puzzle what the difference was, when he suddenly realized it was the light. He went to the window. And saw the town's muddied, filthy streets, ramshackle buildings, and scarred hills had been transformed overnight as though by some fairy's wand. Transformed by a thick layer of snow into a world so white and pure you expected any minute to see an angel go flying by.

And that very second it came to Jimmy what he needed to do.

~~~

Elly wondered at first if Jimmy had taken leave of his senses.

She had finished her coffee and was about to head off to the machine shop. She and Lucas had reduced the Model T Roadster to a pile of parts and a twisted skeleton. But the front axle was made from an alloy so strong it resisted all Lucas's efforts to straighten it, even as it won his admiration. Then he'd wondered if he might gear a steam engine down low enough to supply the power to bend it, and Elly was eager to see if it would work.

She was just putting on her coat when Jimmy came into the kitchen and asked Hannah if he could borrow the toboggan hanging from the rafters of the shed out back.

"Lord, that old thing! Henry got a hold of it somewhere, we used to run down Mineral Hill with it, the winter we were courting. But it's not been used since—" Hannah bit her lip. "Well sure, go ahead. Might need to clean it up first. I've got some beeswax around somewhere..."

"So Elly," Jimmy had said then, "you comin?"

And the way he said it, sort of casual but his eye all feverish—well, she knew she had to go. An hour later they set off, the two of them pulling (by a new rope replacing the one eaten by mice) a freshly oiled and waxed toboggan. Upon which reclined, like a princess on her litter, the heavily-swaddled Moosie.

"You're, you're my HORSES!" she announced. "Giddy up! Go see Santy Claus, lives, lives in a BIG white house"—and much more along those lines.

It was windless, and the sun so bright Elly had to squint. The snow was up to her knees and the going was slow until they got to the main street where horse-drawn sleighs had packed it down. An interurban car with a snowplow attached to the front was slowly advancing down the street and clearing the tracks, a gang of men with shovels following behind.

Jimmy started leading them down a side street. Elly looked a question at him.

"Goin to get Sara and Jonah," he said, not looking at her.

Elly nodded, and smiled to herself.

Sara had cabin fever. Because when it snowed like this, Jonah wished he could be outside playing like the other kids, so he tended to whine. Not a lot—he knew she wouldn't stand for it. But he lay in bed kind of fidgeting and grousing now and then about this and that. Then there was the snow on the roof melting and leaking from the ceiling into three pots and all the *plink-plunk* about to put her around the bend. So when there was a knock on the door, she wasn't in the best frame of mind.

At first she was blinking like mad because it was so bright. But she kept on blinking when she saw it was Jimmy standing there in some silly fur hat, and Elly behind him with not a stylish gown but a pair of overalls peeking from beneath the hem of her coat. Like one of those impossible dreams where people you know are wearing clothing they wouldn't be caught dead in.

"Hey, Sara," said Jimmy.

Jonah yelled out, "Who is it, Sary?" and she turned to shush him. She only had the door open a crack because that's as far as she wanted. In fact she could hardly bear to look at him she was still so angry. She'd hoped so much he'd be different from the rest and treat her like a lady. Because that's still how she felt inside no matter what she'd had to do to survive. But he'd turned out to be just like all the rest of them: looking to buy something she would have given of her own free will when the time was right. And the blame fool couldn't see that making him wait was her way of telling him he was different to her.

Men were just too stupid, she'd finally decided.

So she didn't open the door but a crack. Put her hand on her hip.

"What're you doin here?" she said.

"We's goin tobogganin." He pointed to the other side of the ditch—and if it wasn't an honest-to-God toboggan, and some little girl sitting in it all bundled up like a mummy and staring at her.

She wanted to laugh and cry at the same time. Jonah was yelling, "Sary, Sary who is it?" But she was so flabbergasted, she just waved her hand behind her for him to shush.

"So, uh," said Jimmy, "you comin? You an Jonah?" And said it so sad-like, his eye looking at her all pleading. When he looked at her that way, it did something to her, she just couldn't help herself.

"Y'all are crazy," she said.

But she let them in anyway. Even though she knew what was coming next, and it hurt her heart.

So they all trooped in, Elly leading the little girl by the hand. The little girl stared at Jonah lying on the bed, and he stared back at her; it reminded Sara of two cats meeting. There was a haze of smoke from the leaky stove, and Elly began to cough.

"That there smoke's comin from the stove pipe," said Jimmy, pointing. "You want, I could patch it up."

"Don't need your help," muttered Sara, angry because she couldn't help but see the place through Jimmy and Elly's eyes. By lantern light it hadn't been so bad. But now the roof was leaking, one of Jonah's union suits she could never get the stains out of was hanging above the stove drying, and there was just no hiding how pitiful everything was. And to make it all just cherry-on-top perfect, she was wearing a homespun dress of her mother's, faded to the color of dried flowers, with patches on top of patches and older than she was, her hair was piled up any old way, and she just knew she had ash on her face from fussing with that stove.

All this made her shy for about two seconds. Then, just like before, she decided that if Jimmy wanted to know her, well, here she was. And now he was about to find out everything.

"So, uh, Jonah," said Jimmy, "you ready to go tobogganin?"

Sara could tell he was wondering what this boy was doing still in bed and it's nigh well noon.

"What's tobogganin?" said Jonah.

"It's like a sled, like."

Jonah gaped at him, then looked quickly at Sara. She didn't want to get his hopes up (although it might even work, she was still trying to figure it out). But mostly, she was wondering what Jimmy was going to do when he found out, which would like as not be any second now. Jonah was putting those sad dog eyes on her—oh, he knew how to work her, the devil!—because he could see already she was inclined to give in.

"I can do it, Sary!" He sat up as high as he could. "Just like a sled, he said it is. I can just lie in it, aw come on!"

Elly was staring at what neither of them had noticed in the shadows that night: the shape of Jonah's legs under the blankets. Elly didn't hardly ever talk, but she saw things.

But Jimmy was thick like a man. "Sure, ain't nothin to it," he said. Though Sara could see he was puzzling over what Jonah just said, and she decided it was time to take the bull by the horns.

"See, Jonah's legs don't work too good," she said. Like saying he had a sunburn, or such.

"They's little bitty!" crowed Jonah—and he whipped the blankets off the way he liked to do. She knew he did it this way because it hurt him so to be stared at, and he'd long ago decided it was better to just get it over with. He always put on a show like he didn't care. But she knew he did, and it hurt her every time. Because his legs—well, she was used to it, but they really did look like two skeleton bones.

She had to hand it to Jimmy, because he got over it quicker than most. His eye blinked a couple times, then he said, "Hell, ain't no problem at all. You can ride in the toboggan the whole time, even when we's pullin it up the hill." Smooth as silk.

It made Jonah real happy, and she was glad for him. And the little girl—whose name was Moosie, which is one not-your-run-of-the-mill name for a girl—just went right up and started touching on Jonah's legs through his union suit and said Jonah had chicken legs.

And they all did laugh.

~~~

They headed out of town toward Mineral Hill. Sara had to show them the way. The sun was high in the sky and the world a white wonder. Now and then a sleigh went by with those bells a-jingling so they didn't run a body down, so silent they were otherwise, everything muffled by deep, cottony snow. Jonah and Moosie lay together in the toboggan, Jimmy pulling. She and Elly both offered to help, but even when the snow got deep, he just shook his head. No wind, the sun an oven, and the snow melting fast. It made for perfect snowball weather, and Sara wasn't surprised when the three of them suddenly found themselves being pelted from behind. When Sara was whacked in the head so hard her hat flew off, she turned and fixed Jonah with a look. But it was a funny-angry look, and he only laughed.

Mineral Hill was a great white dome crawling with tiny figures, like ants on a bowl of ice cream. Distant shouts and screams filled the air. They started up the hill, Jimmy still pulling the toboggan. The two kids together weren't enough meal for a mountain lion, but they did add some weight. She asked again if she could help, and again Jimmy shook his head. But a minute later, his face was so red she laughed and grabbed the rope and Elly did too, and the three of them pulled together. And Sara told them—soft so Jonah couldn't hear—about how he fell out of a tree when he was four, and it did something to him so his legs stopped working. And how other things didn't work quite right either so they couldn't stay out too long. Jimmy looked at her blankly, and she realized he had no idea what she was talking about. But she thought Elly did.

The view from the top was fine. The mountains ringing the horizon gleamed silver, and all the valley was a dazzling white but for a few black smokestacks marking the mines. Sara had never ridden a toboggan and told them so, and of course neither had Jimmy nor Elly, so they pretty much had to make it up. They found the only way they would fit was sitting with their legs apart all scrouged up against each other. Moosie rode in front, then Elly, then Jonah on Sara's lap with his legs all wrapped in quilts. Jimmy gave them a running push and jumped on behind with his legs around her. And just like that they were going so fast, the toboggan bumping and thumping over the ground, until by and by they were actually flying through the air for short spells and thudding down on the snow, Moosie screaming in a high funny voice, all of them screaming, even Jimmy.

When they finally smooshed to a stop, Jonah announced it was just the "funnest thing" he'd ever done, Moosie agreed, and so they did it a lot more. Sara had explained to Jimmy how Jonah couldn't feel his legs, so couldn't tell if they were getting froze. So now Jimmy was all the time checking to make sure he was good and bundled up, and it gave her a good feeling. Sometimes she and Jimmy smiled at each other for no reason at all, and when their hands accidentally touched—well even though she was wearing mittens and he thick gloves, it was like a spark flashed between them. So they kept going (even though she was sure Jonah must have had an accident by now). Until they almost ran a boy on a sled down, Jimmy leaned hard to move them out of the way, they flipped over—and suddenly there they were, all lying with their faces in the snow, Moosie bawling, and Jonah laughing his fool head off.

• • •

Back at her cabin, she made hot cocoa (she'd bought some the other day, and wasn't that lucky!). Moosie had a bruise on her forehead and blubbered all the way home, but it seemed she couldn't think of two things at once because the cocoa just knocked the hurt right out of her mind. And Jonah did have an accident, but it seemed like he didn't care and really neither did Sara. She helped him change, and now he and Moosie were on the bed playing some silly game with the blankets and having a high old time. And Sara was sitting on the edge of the bed across the table from Jimmy and Elly like they did that night and feeling pretty good herself, she and Jimmy talking about any old thing—

And then Elly had to open her mouth and spoil it all.

Actually it pretty well spooked Sara every time Elly decided to talk. Really and truly, Sara still couldn't decide what to make of her. Of course she played that piano like a pure angel; it was surely God's gift. But for all that, she seemed at times three bricks short of a full load. Which was funny because Jimmy swore Elly was the smartest person he'd ever met by half.

So she was spooked as usual when Elly started in talking. And double-spooked when the thing she wanted to talk about was Harry Orchard.

"Why're you on about him again?" she said, and all those good feelings she'd been having just flew out the window of her mind. "You know I hate to even think about that time. Wished I never told y'all."

Elly stared into space for a time (Sara thinking how she looked just straight simple when she did that), then said she needed to know exactly what Harry Orchard had said to that other man, the time Sara overheard them. When Sara asked *why* Elly needed to know, she just stared off into space again. Jimmy was trying to signal Sara that he hadn't known Elly was going to ask these things, which helped some. Then finally Elly up and said the one thing that could make Sara want to answer her:

"Because it might help me find who killed your father."

Sara glanced over at Jonah. But Moosie was beating him with a pillow, and Elly talked pretty soft.

So finally Sara sighed and nodded. And sat for a while, collecting herself. "Just remember," she said, "I was only nine years old and what did I know? I only knew Daddy was out of work for the longest time." She took a deep breath. "All right, so it was in June and school was just out, and you know how when school's out, well it's like you're a bird and someone left the door of your cage open—"

She stopped, because she'd gotten this funny feeling.

"Ain't neither of you been to school, has you?"

Elly shook her head, which straight flabbergasted Sara, with all those books she was always reading. Jimmy mumbled he did "a mite," but it never took.

She sighed again, closed her eyes, and thought back to that day. Everything was still so clear in her mind, because after her daddy got killed she'd run it through her head a thousand times, trying to understand it all.

"All right. So school let out, but I didn't go straight home cause I had me this secret place. Found this broken-down old cabin in the woods out near the Vindicator that still had a good stone fireplace and most of its walls. A place where if you was nine years old, you could pretend it was a house and all your own. So that's what I was doin—all alone, cause it was my secret place—brushin at the ground inside the cabin with a pine bough, makin like it was a broom and me a good little housewife.

"So I'm a-brushin away when I hear voices. There's a stove-in window in one of the walls, and I look out this window that ain't there, and I see these two men and one of them is Harry Orchard. They was walkin toward the cabin, so I ducked down behind the wall. But I had enough time to see the other was a gent I didn't know. Wearin a fancy suit and got this big purple spot on his neck a-creepin up on his face the way some people do. So there I am hunkered down below the empty window, and don't they just come and sit down on the other side where there's a log rolled up against the wall of the cabin.

"So I can hear everything they say plain as I can hear you across this table, and when they sit down, Harry's talkin about some train depot. Bout how the graveyard shift comes on at two A.M. so there's lots of miners then standin on the platform. And the gent asks him how many, and Harry says around forty or so, and the gent says that sounds good. Then he says, but it's up to Harry how the thing's done, just tell him what he needs and he'll see he gets it. And Harry says how he needs some dynamite—two boxes he said, I remember it clear—and some caps and somethin about a bottle of acid. And I still didn't think nothin of it because it's just ol Harry Orchard, who likes to fill his pockets with candy and let the kids dig for it. And Daddy talks about blastin all the time, so it just didn't signify nothin to me.

"Then the gent asks how soon he needs the stuff, and Harry says if he got it the next day, he could do the job that night. So the gent says he'll have it and tells him it will be in a wagon parked at such-and-such a spot near some stand of aspen. And Harry says he knows the place.

"And that's all it was," concluded Sara. "They got up and walked away, and I peeked out the window again and saw the gent wearin the city-slicker suit turn his head sideways to say somethin to Harry and got another look at his face. Kinda black-brown hair like a bear and a mustache and dark eyes and that big purple spot like somebody splashed paint on his neck."

Elly was looking straight at her in a way she never did, and Sara could just tell she knew things Sara didn't. So she finished her story. How she heard about the depot explosion two days later, how it was at two in the morning just like they'd talked about and all of those men killed, and she was about sick that she'd known about it before it happened and hadn't said a word. So she told her daddy about what she'd heard, and he asked a few questions about that other gent, and she could see by the way his eyes narrowed the first time she mentioned that purple neck that he knew the man.

"And it was two days after that they came and shot him."

She said it soft. Checked to make sure Jonah wasn't listening, but him and Moosie were playing hide-and-seek under the blankets. Jimmy reached across the table and took hold of her hand. Sara looked at Elly, expecting her to fess up to what she knew.

But she just sat there, spooky as ever.

By December, Elly had played at Crapper Jack's for six months. It was by far the longest she had worked anywhere, and she had achieved a real success. For it was abundantly clear that many people were coming just to hear her; the tables were always full, there was loud applause at the end of each number, and Jack let her play one of her showpieces at the beginning of each set.

Elly was especially renowned for the way she played ragtime. And when she let herself go, the intoxicating swing and lilt she had picked up from old Sam coursing through her slender body and spilling from her fingers, the women without dancing partners had taken to doing a cakewalk together, arching their backs, kicking their legs, and shamelessly showing their stockings. It had made a hit with the customers, and Sam's description of Crapper Jack's as a "regular goldmine" wasn't far off the mark, for her tips often included a gold nugget or two.

Ever since that day in the snow, everything had changed between Jimmy and Sara. It was understood by all the women now that they were sweethearts, and Jimmy had come to an understanding with Jack as well: Sara was not expected to work any "extras," but only to dance—and then only if she cared to (that Jack had given in without a fuss was another measure of Elly's success). Now whenever Sara danced with other men, Jimmy watched her indulgently, and she would wink at him over her partner's shoulder. And she always danced the last waltz with Jimmy. Who—Elly was quite sure—was now supporting her and Jonah.

All this pleased Elly enormously. She was less pleased, however, with the lack of progress with her detective work. For even though

Emma Langdon had found Sara's revelations "most suggestive" (which thrilled Elly; it was the very phrase Sherlock Holmes might have used), she had pointed out that, without the identity of the mysterious man, the case was at a standstill.

Elly had now read—and reread—all the Sherlock Holmes books she could find. In search of more mysteries, she had been delighted to discover the novels of Wilkie Collins, and lay in bed one Sunday evening, her night off, devouring *The Woman in White*. But even as she savored the delicious utterances of the urbanely evil Count Fosco, she kept half an ear on Hannah and Bill's conversation at the kitchen table. For neither had ever discovered how porous the thin wall was (a secret that Elly, with her love of eavesdropping, was in no hurry to reveal).

Abruptly she realized the conversation had taken a serious turn, and was, for a change, being led by Bill. She laid her book aside to focus on his soft voice:

"And, well," he was saying in apologetic tones, "I just don't see how I can meet the payroll this month, Hannah. The ore we're getting now is so low grade it hardly pays to refine it, and coal's so high... I'd lay a few people off, but we're on a skeleton crew as it is."

There was a long silence.

"So I'm afraid," he concluded finally, "I'm afraid I'll just have to give it up."

"Give it up," echoed Hannah in a hollow voice.

Another silence, in which Elly could picture Bill silently nodding.

"Oh Bill, if I could help you—"

"Hannah, this isn't your concern—"

"But I'm only just scraping by myself, the coal's about doing me in this winter too, I don't have a dime to spare—"

"Hannah, please—"

"But what about *us*, Bill? Four years now, I've waited. Tried to believe in your dream. And now you're just...giving up?"

"You know it's not that. If I just had the money to keep on… I feel I'm so *close,* Hannah. I can't tell you why, I just feel it—"

"Oh what's the use of talking about it, Bill? It's all over, isn't it? And…and so are we."

There was a low, plaintive sound, and Elly realized it was Hannah sobbing.

She lay thinking only a moment before coming to a decision.

She and Jimmy both had the habit—acquired as hoboes and reinforced by experiences in theft-prone hotels—of carrying all their money on their persons. She pulled a roll of bills from a pocket she had sewn into the hem of her skirt, and counted out eighteen hundred dollars. Then she put on her robe and slippers and went into the kitchen.

Bill had his arm around Hannah. He looked up at Elly's approach and quickly let go, his face flushing pink. Hannah lifted her head from his shoulder and stared at Elly with red eyes.

Elly sat down and laid the roll of bills in front of Bill.

"Is this enough?"

Bill stared at the money blankly.

"Elly," said Hannah, "what in the world—"

"She heard us," said Bill, his pink skin gone even pinker. "Through the wall."

"Oh Lord," said Hannah, covering her eyes. "And all this time!"

Elly had been afraid of this. In fact it was not the money, but having to reveal her eavesdropping, which had made her hesitate at all.

"It's eighteen hundred dollars," she said. "Is it enough?"

Bill was silent for a long moment. "Well, yes I suppose it would be," he finally admitted. "But Elly, I could never take your money."

Elly was brought up short by Bill's refusal. Beyond having enough for food, clothing, and housing, money had never meant that much to her. A stubborn resolve seized her: she would not leave the table until Bill accepted her money.

"You need this money, and I don't," she said simply.

For the next twenty minutes, Bill and Hannah fought with her. As inarticulate as always, Elly settled on the tactic of repeating herself, over and over—"You need this money, and I don't"—and every time Bill pushed the money toward her, she pushed it right back.

Finally Bill leaned back in his chair and ran his hands through his thinning blonde hair, exasperated. Elly stared at the table, stone-faced and defiant. Hannah held her face in her hands, shaking her head and laughing somewhat hysterically.

"Well," said Bill finally, "the only way I'll accept this is as a loan. All drawn up and legal. And even if the mine goes bust, I'll make enough selling my equipment to pay you back. You have my word on that, Elly."

He reached across the table and solemnly shook her hand. "You're a hard person to argue with," he added, smiling in spite of himself. Elly felt proud and rather adult. Hannah jumped up, came around the table, took her by the shoulders and leaned down to whisper in her ear:

"You are really something."

Time passed, and the urgency of Elly's stillborn investigation faded. Until one evening in late December when everything changed.

It was three days before Christmas and all the miners from Hannah's boarding house were at Crapper Jack's, crowded around the table nearest the piano, continuing the farewell party for Eli Stanton that had begun with that evening's dinner. The young prospector had fulfilled Pinky's prophecy that he would run back home to Yale when he tired of mining, and was leaving tomorrow on the morning train. Hannah had cooked a special dinner of roast venison and mince pie, and now Eli was the good-natured butt of a hundred jokes as he stood the miners drinks.

Elly watched it all from the piano; watched especially Bill Wynn, who spoke and drank very little, but smiled at all the jests (and now and then smiled at Elly, making her blush). Jimmy sat down with them, and tried to call Sara over to be introduced. But she was suddenly shy, and shook her head.

Eli had bought a roll of dance tickets for the miners. Harold Baxter was the first to get up and dance with blousy, hennaed Helma, breaking away from her in the middle of a polka to demonstrate some English music hall steps. Then old Pinky pulled mannish Mamie out onto the dance floor, and the things he whispered in her ear as he bounced her around the room against his belly made her laugh so hard they staggered and almost fell.

Elly began a new waltz that was all the rage entitled "When It's Springtime in the Rockies," even though spring seemed awfully far away. She noticed Zachary Crabbe trying to get Sara to take his dance ticket. She shook her head, and his pimply face went slack. Jimmy tapped her on the shoulder and presented his dance ticket with a grin. She slapped at his hand, laughing, then stepped into his arms. A moment later they were gracefully circling the room (with all his practice, Jimmy now danced quite well) while Crabbe looked on mournfully.

Then Elly lost herself in the music for a time, only to feel someone tapping on her ankle. There was nothing she so hated as being touched while she was playing. She looked down, annoyed—and discovered Jimmy looking back up at her from below the stage with the strangest expression. His arm was around Sara. She stood with her face in her hands, shaking her head convulsively.

Elly finished a chorus, tacked on an ending, and leaned over the stage.

"It's that feller," said Jimmy. "The feller with the purple neck. He's here."

"Are you sure?" said Elly.

Without lifting her face from her hands, Sara nodded. Jimmy was motioning with his head toward a man sitting alone at the bar, far down at the end near the door. Elly still had twenty minutes left in her set. She frowned, thinking.

"Watch him," she ordered Jimmy. "If he leaves, follow him." She turned back to play again, then added over her shoulder, "but don't let him see you."

Jimmy squeezed Sara's shoulder and whispered something in her ear, then sauntered to the bar and sat a couple stools down from the man. The bartender was too busy to gab and besides saying, "Beer, Jimmy?" and pouring him one, left him alone. Which was good because he was trying not to draw attention to himself. He'd been forced to sit with the man on the side of his eye patch and had to look in the mirror behind the bar to study him. He'd been doubtful at first (even though Sara had gone white at the sight of him and turned to stone in Jimmy's arms; it had been like dancing with a dead person). For Sara had described the gent she'd seen with Harry Orchard as a sharp dresser, and this man was about dressed for hoboing. His suit was shiny at the elbows and the cuffs frayed, and beside him lay a ragged overcoat and misshapen fedora; Jimmy was almost surprised Curly had let him in the bar.

But the man didn't seem to hear the music or notice anything, just stared into space, so Jimmy was able to study him plain; saw the dark eyes and hair (growing gray at the edges now)—but most of all that god-awful purple neck creeping above his dirty collar like a stain fixing to spread over his whole face.

Suddenly the man tossed down the rest of his drink, reached for his coat and battered fedora, and left. Jimmy glanced across the room. Elly was pounding out a polka, but both she and Sara were anxiously watching him. He nodded toward them, grabbed his hat and coat, and rushed out the door.

He spotted the man a half block away and followed behind him. It was colder than that South Pole Pinky and Lars were always going on about, and he was thankful when, a couple of blocks later, the man ducked into the Lords Saloon. Jimmy waited a minute, tried to stroll in all casual-like without being noticed, and spotted the man again sitting at the bar. But the place was half empty, the man glanced at him with mild surprise—and Jimmy realized his damn eye patch was as good as having a purple neck.

He tried to make like it was all just chance and sat down at a table across the room. The bartender was pouring the man another whiskey. A girl sashayed over and asked Jimmy what he'd like, giving him a look that made it two questions. He ordered another beer, and looked back at the man.

Just in time to see him walk out the door.

Feeling like a fool, he threw some money on the table and rushed after him. The man was turning the corner onto Main. Jimmy ran after him, then stopped, realizing he'd better be double-careful. He peered slowly around the last building and about froze his nose off, the wind whistling down the street was that cold. The man was bent forward and pulling at the collar of his ragged coat as he walked into the arctic blast. It was after eleven, the street almost deserted. From behind both of them came the low rumble of the interurban, making a late run. The man turned around. Jimmy pulled the brim of his derby down and looked toward the ground to hide his eye patch.

The electric car rounded a bend, and its light made the snowdrifts glisten. The man waved his arm and it slowed to a stop.

Now Jimmy had a tough call. There were only a few people in the well-lit car, and he'd surely be spotted. Almost without thinking the old hobo skills took over, and as the car began to move, he ran behind and jumped onto the back. In the excitement of the chase he'd neglected to put on his gloves, and the cold metal burned his hands. Clinging with one hand at a time, he managed to wriggle them on and pull his derby down tight over his ears. His coat flapped behind him as the car picked up speed, and he cursed the vanity that had made him wear a thin but well-cut suit on a night like this.

He was wondering if he'd even make it to wherever they were going before he turned into a block of ice. But at the edge of town the car suddenly slowed, and the man got off. Jimmy judged the unlit streets dark enough and jumped off a moment later. The man began climbing a side street that led up a steep incline. Visible at the top were the lights of a mansion. Jimmy had noticed it before (hard not to, since it was by far the biggest house in Cripple). With five turrets—one on each corner and one in the center—it reminded him of a castle, and commanded a spectacular view of the town, even as it demanded notice from the town as well.

The man trudged up the hill with the wind flapping at his coattails, and Jimmy followed behind. The night was moonless, starless, utterly black but for the lights burning far above them, and Jimmy was pretty near invisible. The hill was steep, the road icy. Twice the man slipped, and Jimmy guessed he was the worse for drink.

The mansion was even more imposing up close. Jimmy watched as the man ascended the front porch, then stood a long moment as if gathering courage. Finally he knocked. After a minute the door opened. The man's shoddy appearance obviously worked against him, because a few moments later the door shut in his face. But his message must have been relayed, because after another long wait he was finally ushered inside.

Jimmy got closer and tried peering into windows, but they were all frosted over. He found a corner of the house that sheltered him from the wind, pulled his collar up, and settled down to wait.

It seemed endless. The cold seeped into him like an evil, live thing. He clapped his hands, hugged himself, danced a jig. Several times he was about to pack it in. But the thought of Sara's face at the news he'd given up kept him there. Still, there came a time—he'd stood there nigh on two hours, he reckoned, and was shivering to make his teeth rattle—when he decided the man must be staying the night and started down the hill to beat it for home.

At that moment there was a noise behind him. He turned, saw the door opening, and threw himself down in the snow. A minute later the man came lurching unsteadily by, and Jimmy realized if he hadn't been drunk before, he surely was now.

At the bottom of the hill he staggered off in the direction of town, Jimmy following behind. Never once did the man look back, his erratic forward motion fueled by both whiskey, and—it seemed to

Jimmy—anger. Jimmy's own feet were numb, and his teeth chattered. His thoughts came slow as cold molasses, and he supposed his brain must be frozen as well. The wind made his eye patch flap, and his face felt hard as a mask.

When they reached the business part of town, the man entered a cheap hotel. As Jimmy stood in the empty street, staring stupidly at the door through which he had disappeared, the wind suddenly increased in fury. And it was at that instant, Jimmy later decided, that the very soul was sucked out of him.

He turned and staggered for home.

Chapter Seven

Investigations

When Jimmy still hadn't come down by noon the next day, Elly went upstairs and knocked on his door. Getting no answer, she let herself inside. Jimmy lay in bed. The room stank of sweat, and she saw his face was slick with perspiration. The quilt covering his chest rose and fell with the labor of breathing. She said his name, and his eye slowly opened a crack.

"Elly," he croaked, "I's sicker than a dog, I am."

Elly nodded—it was plain.

Jimmy's eye closed. His breath came in gasps. In the same ruined voice, he said:

"I saw him go into that…that big castle-like kinda house. Up on the hill." He stopped. His eye opened again and looked up at Elly. She nodded and it closed. "Stayed there couple hours. Then he, he, he went back to…some cheap hotel." A coughing fit seized him. When it subsided, he lay panting. Sweat trickled down the sides of his face. "On Myers…cross from that café…gr-gr-green sign," he said, biting off the words.

Elly watched him for a long time, until it seemed he was asleep. She reached down and stroked his damp forehead. His eye opened again.

"You'll…you'll run him to ground, won't yer, Elly?"

She nodded.

Hannah and Moosie were just returning from the market when she came back downstairs.

"Lord in heaven," muttered Hannah. She slammed the door with her foot, dropped her basket, and rushed to the stove to warm herself. "Thirty below at least. I pity those poor vendors, even with their braziers—come here, Moosie, let's get those things off—" She broke off suddenly at the sight of Elly's face.

"Jimmy's sick."

Hannah stared at her, then clumped upstairs, trailed by Moosie, both of them still in their coats.

Elly dressed as warmly as she could: two sets of long johns and two pairs of wool socks, heavy woolen dress, two sweaters, coat and scarf. She reached for the oversized woolen stocking she'd been using for a cap, then had another thought and went back upstairs.

She found Hannah applying a towel wrapped around some snow to Jimmy's burning forehead as Moosie looked on dispassionately.

"Oh he's sick all right, I'm calling the doctor. Pneumonia, I'm just sure of it."

Elly thought of the many times, while reciting the backdoor spiel he had perfected during their hoboing days, Jimmy had blithely killed off his whole family ("Ma and Pa and poor lil Matilda too") with the "pneumonyer," and her heart did a little flip. She looked around the room, found Jimmy's bear-fur hat, and tried it on. Moosie laughed, delighted.

"I have to go out," she said.

Hannah regarded her for a long moment, then nodded.

"Don't worry," she said, "I'll watch him."

Though Jimmy had been unable to read the name of the hotel, his description had been accurate enough. And four hours later, Elly sat in the café nursing yet another cup of coffee, her eye fixed on the ramshackle façade of a building across the street whose sign, in faded green letters, proclaimed it to be—against all outward evidence—the Grand Hotel.

She was filled with conflicting feelings: excitement that the mystery seemed on the verge of being solved; concern for Jimmy (and guilt that, by ordering him around, she had been the unwitting agent of his illness); but most of all, boredom. If only she had thought to organize, like Sherlock Holmes, a band of street Arabs for jobs like hotel-watching, her own "Cripple Creek Irregulars." But street Arabs were in short supply when the temperature was thirty below zero, and Elly was dismally aware that her organizational skills were on a par with her ability to make small talk.

This second shortcoming could also be a problem for a detective, as she'd already discovered in two interviews that day. First with the clerk of the hotel, a grubby man with a luxuriant mustache and equally impressive paunch she found lounging by a coal stove in suspenders and carpet slippers like an indolent walrus.

"Yeeaah," he said, yawning at her approach and rubbing his eyes. "What?"

Elly laid a five dollar gold piece on the counter with what she hoped was a certain panache. The man's reaction was to yawn even wider. But his eyes were on the money as he eased himself to his feet.

"Can you tell me the name of the man with the purple neck?"

The clerk rubbed the sleep from his face and snatched the coin up in one smooth motion.

"Why you wanna know?" he drawled.

Elly just stared at him (or rather at some egg yolk adorning the tip of his mustache, avoiding his eye).

"Okey dokey, have it your way," shrugged the clerk. He opened the register, ran a fat finger down the page, and nodded. "That's him." He rotated the ledger so Elly could read.

She studied it for a long time but could make nothing of it. "What does it say?" she finally asked.

"Hey now, for that it'll cost ya another five bucks."

Only when the man began to chuckle did she realize it was a joke. She had another question ready.

"When he comes and goes, can you make a note of the times? And if he has any visitors?"

"Well now," said the clerk, now fully awake, "that really does seem like more than our original bargain." He smiled at her in an oily kind of way, and Elly realized she should have held on to the money until the end. With a sigh she laid another five dollars on the counter.

"Okey dokey," said the clerk—and whisked the coin away like a conjuror.

Her second interview had taken place at the mansion Jimmy had described.

Elly remembered it well. She had even asked Bill and Hannah about it once as the three of them sat at the kitchen table drinking tea, for they often invited her now to join them (whether this was due to her new status as Bill's benefactor, or the fact that she could hear them anyway through the wall, Elly wasn't quite sure). At any rate, she'd learned the mansion belonged to Charlie Tutt, owner of several mines, including the big Vindicator.

"You remember, Elly," said Bill. "He was Grand Marshall of the Fourth of July parade. Rode in the motorcar up front—that's his as well."

Elly only dimly remembered the fat man with the red sash across his chest and the uniformed and goggled chauffeur, for all her attention had been on the lovely Pierce-Arrow.

"Only one of those rich mine owners who cares to live in Cripple," sniffed Hannah. "All the rest built big houses in Colorado Springs."

"Yeah, I'll give Charlie that," said Bill, nodding—it seemed to Elly—somewhat reluctantly. "He didn't build it, though. Man who did was an attorney named Finn. Got rich settling competing claims.

Back when Teddy Roosevelt was vice president, he was planning a visit to Cripple, and Finn wanted a place fit to hold a reception for him. Got it built in record time, had a slam-bang party for Teddy—then went bankrupt. Tutt picked it up for a song."

Elly took the interurban to the foot of the hill upon which the mansion roosted, and began the steep climb to the top. Wind whistled down the hill as though it were a bowling alley and she a pin. She felt her cheeks begin to freeze, and thought of Jimmy standing outside the house for hours.

Close up it was even bigger and more imposing. Ice had frozen on the windows into delicate patterns like cut glass. She climbed the front steps and was standing before the massive oak door when the enormity of what she was about to do suddenly overwhelmed her.

Perhaps it would be better to reconnoiter, she thought.

Smoke—visible for an instant before the wind snatched it away—was coming from the roof of a nearby coach house. She wandered over to the large double doors and peered in a window. Through the ice, she could make out a glow of rich forest-green.

She found a side-door and let herself in. She had been right: it was the Pierce-Arrow. A man with curly red hair, wearing green uniform pants, a shapeless sweater, and smoking a cigarette, broke off from waxing the lovely automobile to stare at her. She guessed he must be the chauffeur who'd driven it in the parade.

"Well hey now," he said, smiling. He was good-looking, in an Irish kind of way, with a hint of brogue to his speech. "And what can I be doin for ya?"

Elly thought it would be a good idea this time to break the ice with some small talk. She pointed to the engine housing.

"In-line six cylinder," she said in her toneless voice. "Five inch bore, seven inch stroke. Makes a bore/stroke ratio of point seven one."

The man stared at her wide-eyed—then pulled the cigarette from his lips to let out an enormous laugh.

"You must," he said, still chuckling, "you must know Lucas."

Elly nodded, pleased that the ice-breaking had gone so nicely.

"Do you know a man with a purple neck?" she asked.

The man looked puzzled. "A sort of riddle, is it?"

Elly shook her head.

"Well now," he said, rubbing his chin, "can't say that I do."

Elly tried to think of another question, but could come up with nothing.

"Good-bye," she said.

"Well it's good-bye, is it—and here you've only just arrived! Just like a woman," added the man, smiling at her. She did her best to smile back, then left out the side door and headed back toward the house. But the big mansion looked more intimidating than ever.

She decided to go back and watch the hotel.

So here she was, sitting in a café and drinking too much coffee. It was already growing dark; soon she would have to return to the boarding house and get dressed for the evening. It was all so discouraging—

The door of the hotel opened, and the man with the purple neck rushed out, still buttoning his coat and pulling his hat and scarf tight. Elly jumped up—she'd made sure to pay for each cup of coffee when it came, she'd done one thing right at least—and hurried out of the café. The man was almost running down the street and, to Elly's surprise, in the opposite direction from Charlie Tutt's house. He strode forward purposefully, paying little attention to his surroundings, and she was able to follow close behind with little danger of discovery.

It was almost dark, the dirty snow and dull gray sky somehow in harmony with the bitter cold. After three blocks he turned down a narrow side street. Beyond a furniture upholsterer and a livery stable was an area of modest houses. The man paused for a moment before a run-down place with a "For Rent" sign on the window as if gathering resolve, then walked up the steps to the front porch. The door was unlocked, and he entered without knocking.

Elly had no choice but to take up a post nearby and wait for developments. The house had looked deserted, but through the gloom she could make out smoke coming from a metal stove pipe, and a dim light glowed in one of the rear windows. She had just time to notice these things when there was a sound like a clap of thunder.

A sound that could only have been one thing.

She rushed across the street and up the porch steps to the door—then froze with her hand on the knob at the muffled sound of horse's hooves on snow. She ran to the side of the porch in time to see a man on a chestnut mare galloping away from her down the alley. He turned a corner and was gone.

She returned to the door, gathered her courage, and pushed it open. She called out "Hello," but expected no answer and received none. She stepped inside. The front room was in deep shadow, but she could still see it was empty. An acrid smell hung in the air. A hazy, smoky light spilled from an open doorway leading into the kitchen. Almost against her will, like a moth to an open flame, she felt herself being drawn toward it...

The force of the blast had knocked both him and his chair backward, and his body was splayed on the floor at a grotesque angle. The chair had been seated at a small table. A kerosene lantern on the table cast a warm glow on the ghastly tableau. No purple neck now; in fact no neck at all. Red stew of hair and brains. Red splattered on floor and wall...

Elly felt her mind separate into two parts. One was almost numb with horror. The other began calmly issuing orders.

"Look at everything," it was saying. "No—not at that. Look at everything *but* that. Look—and remember."

So she looked. There was a small satchel lying on the table beside the lamp. She stepped around the body and looked inside; it was stuffed full of old newspapers. She glanced quickly at them and decided their content held no significance. There was a fire in the stove. She judged it to have been going for less than an hour, for the surfaces of the room were still cold. Next to the stove was a chair and on the floor beside it a pile of cigarette butts; she counted five.

She stepped out the back door and saw the beaten snow and pile of droppings where the horse had been tied up. She stood still a moment, trying not to listen to the voice inside her, sick with loathing at what it was now telling her to do.

"Go back inside and search his pockets. Don't think about it—just do it."

So she did, stuffing what odds and ends she found, unexamined, into the pockets of her coat. Then she hurried away.

She followed the tracks of the horse down the alley, then stopped suddenly to vomit into the snow, sickened by the difference between the thrilling descriptions of such scenes in the books she read, and the awful sordidness of the real thing. She continued on, but as she had expected, the trail led back to the main street and was lost in the confusion of tracks in the snow.

She trudged on in a sort of daze, insensible of the cold, hardly a thought in her head. When she passed the hotel, it occurred to her vaguely that the clerk might be able to tell her something. She found him dozing in front of the stove in the exact attitude as before, as if everything that had happened had yet to occur, and despaired of learning anything important from him.

In this she would be surprised.

"Well now," said the clerk after she had managed to rouse him. "I just thought you'd want to know why he hot-footed it like that. So I listened close and wrote it all down."

Elly gazed at him, confused.

"It was a telephone call. Just had one installed," he said, pointing to a wooden box mounted on the wall across from the desk. "And lucky for you. First off, his name's Bemore. But the fella on the other end had to mention the spot on his neck, or I wouldn't of known who to call down."

"Who was it?" asked Elly.

"Who was it called him? Well now, I can't say exactly. But his first name was Charlie. Here," he said eagerly, turning a pad of paper in her direction so she could read what he'd written. "Wrote it all down exact."

Hello well youve come round have you
yep yep sure I can find it yep yep
you won't regret this Charlie
I swear I'll never bother you again

"Uh-huh, all just exactly like he said it," the clerk was saying. "Every word." He paused. "Worth another five bucks, wouldn't you say?"

She got to the boarding house with barely enough time to change for her job. But first, she ran upstairs to check on Jimmy and tell him the news. Jimmy's face was pale and translucent. His mouth hung open, and his breath came in long, labored wheezes. His chest was encased in some sort of cast that gave off a sharp odor. She said his name, but he made no answer. A half-empty bottle of medicine (the sort her old mentor Professor Carp would have enjoyed) sat on the side table.

"It's pneumonia, all right," said Hannah when Elly found her in the kitchen. "Doctor came and went. Not much we can do but let it run its course. He's a young, strong boy, Elly," she added, stroking Elly's cheek.

Elly nodded and went to get dressed. Because she did not like people to see her cry.

That night Elly was stunned to discover that—for the first time in her life—that magical ability she had to lose herself in her playing had evaporated. Instead, her fingers moved like automatons over the keys as her mind obsessively ran over the day's events.

On her break, she sat with Sara and told her what had happened. But Sara hardly seemed to register the death of the man whose memory had haunted her all these years, and it was Jimmy's plight which filled her with concern. And a remorse that Elly knew should rightly be hers alone.

"Oh Elly," said Sara, sitting across from her and kneading one of Elly's hands between both of hers, "why'd I ever mention any of that fool stuff? I should of known nothin good could ever come of it."

Miserably Elly reflected that it was *she* who had pulled the story out of Sara.

"You care bout him too, don't you?" said Sara.

Elly began to weep.

"Oh Elly, Elly." Sara squeezed her hand convulsively. "I knew it — I knew you must see him like I do! Such a good heart he has, don't he? Even if," she added, smiling through her own tears, "even if he does like to brag and strut some."

They sat a while longer, neither of them speaking, but their hands continuing a kind of conversation.

"When can I see him?" said Sara, breaking the silence. "Oh they just gotta let me see him…"

"Elly, I'm just so sorry. But I don't care how thick they are, I will not have Jimmy's, Jimmy's *floozie* in my boarding house."

Hannah stood before Elly with her hand on her hip. Her gray eyes were hard and unyielding. Elly felt her face flush and looked at the floor in confusion. Hannah turned back to her cooking, talking over her shoulder.

"Look, I'm sure she's maybe a nice girl, but — no, no it's impossible. She'll just have to wait until he gets better. Which I'm sure he will," she added. And began chopping an onion in a way that said the conversation was over.

But Jimmy was not getting better, though Hannah was doing all she could. Zachary Crabbe had been banished to the horsehair sofa in the parlor, the coal stove in the dining room was kept well-stoked so the pipe running along the wall of Jimmy's bedroom would take the chill away, hot bricks were regularly ferried from the stove to be placed under his bedding, and both Elly and Hannah rubbed his forehead regularly with camphor oil. But it still looked like someone had substituted a wax dummy for the real Jimmy, and made a poor job of it.

Elly scanned the local paper and found a brief article about an unknown man killed by a shotgun blast in an empty house on Placer Street. The assailants were believed to be a man and a boy, who escaped on horseback. The police were making enquiries.

She brooded on this boy for several minutes before she realized it was her own bloody footprints they had found.

She had taken several things from Bemore's pockets: a half-smoked cigar and box of matches; a torn, one-way ticket from Colorado Springs to Cripple Creek dated the day they had seen him in the bar; a pamphlet entitled "The Great Love of Jesus"; a dirty handkerchief; four crumpled dollar bills and seventy-three cents in change; and a prospectus advertising properties in French Polynesia.

Both printed items were soiled and heavily creased, and she examined them carefully. The religious pamphlet was crudely printed, and after reading it through, Elly decided the gist of its argument was that belief in Jesus gave one magical powers. An anecdote about a man whose acceptance of Christ led directly to a monetary windfall was heavily underlined in pencil.

The prospectus was a much more slickly-produced item, with a cover graced by a color lithograph of a palm-studded estate. On the verandah of its well-appointed bungalow a man reclined indolently, frozen in the act of plucking a fruit from a bowl held by a bare-breasted native girl. The inside pages contained descriptions of various properties, with prices ranging from a few hundred to many thousands of dollars. Again, many of these were heavily underlined. In one of the margins was a penciled scrawl: "SF—Haw—Tah 2nd $138 St $98."

Elly tried to apply the deductive methods of Sherlock Holmes to this trove of clues.

Since no one she'd asked had known of a purple-necked man, she had already decided that Bemore must have left Cripple Creek soon after Sara's father was murdered; the train ticket supported this idea. She further guessed that he'd meant to leave again after his business here was finished, and had not bought a return ticket simply because—as his clothing, choice of lodging, and the paltry sum in his pocket all attested—he was at the end of his luck.

The two pamphlets suggested Bemore believed his luck was about to change. But Elly judged the Christian tract far-fetched, the Polynesian prospectus too good to be true, and any man who set much stock in them to be an impractical dreamer. She wondered if this character flaw had led to Bemore's ruin; an addiction to gambling would have been consistent. The figures scrawled in the margin of the prospectus were obviously second class and steerage prices for passage on a steamer from San Francisco to Tahiti via Hawaii. And attested to Bemore's pathetic confidence that his own ship was about to come in.

But the exact nature of his plan still eluded Elly. And she decided it was time for another visit to Emma Langdon.

Elly sat in the same chair, the golden eagle lurking over her shoulder. Emma had by now grown used to her ways and sat quietly, letting her tell the story in her own halting manner without interrupting. She listened to the details of what Sara had overheard, examined the sheet of paper on which the clerk had transcribed Bemore's telephone conversation, as well as the two pamphlets, nodding her head at Elly's deductions. At the conclusion of her story Emma still said nothing. Finally she gave a deep sigh.

"Well Elly, I must say, I *am* impressed. You have the makings of a first-class detective."

Elly glowed.

"And your conclusions strike me as all quite sound. It's only the final conclusion you have yet to draw. After all, by what possible method could such a pathetic creature as this Bemore ever hope to strike it rich?"

"Blackmail?" murmured Elly.

"Blackmail," agreed Emma. "And with what? With Bemore's intimate knowledge of what we have suspected all along: it was the mine owners who put Harry Orchard up to his terrible deeds. Oh Elly," she exclaimed, gathering heat, "can you imagine? A man willing to murder the workers in his own mines so the union would be blamed! For it was in Charlie Tutt's own Vindicator that those fifteen men fell to their deaths. And most of the men who died in the Independence Depot explosion were getting off shifts at his mines as well.

"As for this man Bemore, he was—as you have discovered—nothing. One of Tutt's lackeys, a mere go-between. Your friend's father recognized him; I'm sure if you'd asked more people, you would have found other men who remembered him. And after he left town and fell on hard times, he hit on the desperate plan of blackmailing Tutt.

"A fool, Elly! Would a man who could kill a score of his own men so callously, and have your friend's father murdered in cold blood before his entire family—would such a man hesitate to murder again to save his own hide? A fool, as I said. Who went to that deserted house, looked inside that satchel expecting to see a stack of money—and at that moment the world was rid of one more fool.

"And now, Elly," Emma burst out, "*I'm* the fool!" She jumped up, and the eagle's eyes seemed to follow her as she began pacing around the room. "A prize fool to ever have encouraged you in this way! Pure vanity on my part, and idle curiosity, I suppose. Well now my curiosity's satisfied"—she sat down again and fixed Elly with a terrible stare—"and you and your friend are in *deadly peril.*"

Elly stared at her.

"Just think: Tutt has murdered the only two people he thought could connect him to Harry Orchard. But if he should ever find out that your friend was the *true* witness..."

Elly felt her blood run cold.

"Oh yes. This is what capitalism breeds, you see, Elly. For the end result of the acquisition of obscene wealth is unlimited, corrupting power. And we have no way of knowing how far the plot went. Was it only Tutt? Or was he, as the only big mine owner still living in Cripple Creek, merely acting on behalf of the others? Or could the thing—it's not impossible—lead all the way to the governor's mansion?"

She paused, then reached out to take hold of Elly's hands. "And so," she said in a quiet but compelling voice, "you've got a tiger by the tail, Elly. A very large, very dangerous tiger. And you must promise me—*promise me!*—you'll let go of it and run as fast as you can in the other direction. Forget all about our investigation. Will you?"

Elly could only nod mutely.

~~~

As she rode the interurban back to Cripple Creek, Elly brooded on Emma's words. What kind of world was it where a man like Tutt could go unpunished? But the danger to Sara—and to herself, who now shared the secret—was very real.

She made a solemn vow to herself to honor her promise and abandon all her detective fantasies.

Outside the window the weather had finally cleared, and though it was still bitterly cold, a brilliant blue sky held a promise of the sun's warming rays. She closed her eyes, tried to put all that terrible business from her mind, and concentrated instead on composing the speech she had decided to make.

She found Hannah upstairs with Jimmy. The doctor had removed the mustard plaster cast from his chest, and she was rubbing it with camphor oil. Elly felt ashamed that, absorbed in her investigation, she had not been doing more for Jimmy herself. One look at him was enough to see he was no better. And wouldn't hear what she was about to say.

Hannah was telling the story of Moosie's latest escapade (something about her tunneling into the snow and being almost suffocated when the result collapsed on her), but broke off when she noticed the fixed and peculiar look on Elly's normally expressionless face.

"Elly, what is it?"

"You have to let Sara come," said Elly.

Hannah sighed and rolled her eyes. "Elly, I've said all I have to say—"

"You're wrong."

Hannah stopped rubbing Jimmy and stared at her.

"You can be a whore and still be a good person," continued Elly. "Sara was a whore because her parents are both dead and she had no other way to support herself and her little brother. But she's not a whore anymore; she only dances with the men now because Jimmy's supporting her. Because they're in love."

Hannah continued to stare at Elly, her jaw slowly dropping.

"And," continued Elly, tonelessly but relentlessly, "you loved Liddie—even though you knew she became a whore."

Hannah blushed scarlet.

"And so," Elly concluded, "you have to admit the possibility that you could be wrong about Sara."

"But," stammered Hannah, "but how did you—?"

Elly had remembered Hannah's discomfort when she talked of Liddie moving out of her boarding house after little Sam's murder. Remembered her saying she had waved at Liddie on the street, but she had looked away. And was sure, by the way Hannah had told the story, she had known very well what had become of Liddie, but was too prudish to tell.

But all this was not part of Elly's prepared speech, and she could only stand there, helpless. Hannah had a hand over her eyes and was shaking her head. Suddenly she bounded up from the bedside and enveloped Elly in a fierce, clumsy hug.

"Oh Lord, Elly," she murmured into Elly's ear, stroking her hair. "You have shown me for the hypocrite I am." She grasped Elly's shoulders and looked her in the eye.

"Tell her she can come."

Chapter Eight

Today's the Day

Sara came the next afternoon.

She wore a rather dowdy but respectable frock Elly suspected she had purchased for the occasion, and sat by Jimmy's bedside, stroking his face and speaking softly to him as Elly and Hannah looked on. The sound of her voice must have penetrated his fevered brain, for after a while his chest began to heave and he murmured, "Sara?"

"Yeah, it's me, Jimmy," cried Sara, kissing him on the forehead and hugging him. Tears streamed down her face, and Elly noticed Hannah's eyes were misty as well. But Jimmy's lucidity was short-lived, and though Sara sat with him for another hour, the fever had reclaimed him.

Sara consented to have a cup of tea with Hannah. But speech between the two women was stiff and formal for a while, and Sara refused Hannah's polite invitation to stay for supper, saying she had to "get back to Jonah." Moosie had wandered into the kitchen and asked if Jonah's legs had "got any bigger," and Sara had smiled and said no, they "prob'ly never would." Hannah was curious so Sara began to explain—and it was like ice jamming a river suddenly breaking free, such a torrent of conversation rushing between the two women that Elly got dizzy listening.

Sara began to come every day, and consented to bring Jonah over for Sunday dinner. Elly helped her haul him over in the toboggan, and Sara carried him upstairs on her back to see Jimmy.

"So Jonah," said Hannah brightly as Sara placed him in a chair next to the bed, "Sara tells me you have a little trouble walking?"

"Cain't walk a'tall," replied Jonah cheerfully, pulling up a loose pant leg to display his skeletal physique. "They's little bitty. Only way to get em to move is grab em and move em around, like I'm a puppet."

Hannah nodded matter-of-factly at this information, but Elly could see something in her eyes. Jimmy had been improving all week, and roused himself enough to remark that now he got to laze around in bed all day like Jonah, which made Jonah laugh. Then Jimmy soberly added that being as how he, Jimmy, was "out of action for a spell," it was up to Jonah to take care of Sara. Jonah gravely nodded, and Sara rolled her eyes.

At the dinner table they wedged Jonah into a chair piled with cushions, and he ate so much of Hannah's roast chicken and peach cobbler that Elly had to wonder about Sara's cooking. Later he fell asleep on Elly's bed, and Hannah suggested Sara and Elly join her and Bill in the kitchen for a cup of hot tea before they hauled Jonah back to Sara's place. They were just sitting down when Zachary Crabbe poked his nose into the kitchen, then stood there, looking uncomfortable. Elly had noticed him furtively peering at Sara all through the dinner, and so was not as shocked as the others when he accepted Hannah's polite invitation to join them. She *was* surprised, though, when the painfully shy youth suddenly put down his teacup in the middle of a story Bill was telling and addressed Sara:

"Hey," he said, "how come you to work at Crapper Jack's, anyhow?"

Sara stared at him a long moment. "You askin me," she said finally, "what manner of woman chooses to be a whore?"

Crabbe's mouth fell open, displaying his long goat teeth. The kitchen had gone utterly silent. Hannah blushed a deep pink, opened her mouth to change the subject—but Sara held up a hand to stop her.

"That's all right," she said. "He wants to know. I was curious too, when I first started in workin there, and so I studied on it some."

She was silent a moment, organizing her thoughts, and when she finally began to speak, it was in matter-of-fact tones: "Well, I come to think there's several different kinds. First," she continued, counting on her fingers, "your most common whore is just uncommon lazy. I mean, your respectable life—your cookin, cleanin, baby-birthin—well it's all hard work, ain't it?"

She glanced at Hannah, who gave a tiny nod.

"So these girls has took the easy way out. And when I say lazy, I declare ain't nobody could be as lazy as they without they had years of practice.

"Then they's the greedy ones. Cause they's money to be made, a girl wants to work at it. Some spends it all on fancy dresses and gewgaws. But some's scratchin and scrapin to open a hat shop or some other pie-in-the sky dream. And by and by some of em even does.

"Then"—Sara counted off another finger—"they's some that likes the drink and such-like things, and lyin on they backs is just the easiest way to pay for it. And some that—well, I got to say it—they's some that just likes it too much. The men."

She raised her eyebrows significantly. Hannah was now blushing so deeply her ears had turned red.

"And they's a lot," continued Sara, "a lot of girls that—well, they had no choice. Got put in the family way by sweethearts that promised to marry em—then sort of forgot. Or got interfered with by their daddies or uncles, and decided they ain't fit for nothin else."

Hannah let out an involuntary gasp, and Bill reached over to squeeze her hand.

Sara hugged herself for a moment, then continued on in a new voice:

"And then they's some that's just weak. Like life's a fast-moving stream, and they just little bitty leaves gettin swirled about every which way, and they just had the bad luck to get washed up in the wrong place.

"And one of these—a girl I know—well, she's a girl lost her parents and don't have no family she knows how to find and can't cook nor sew hardly a lick, though the Lord knows she did try."

Sara's eyes were glistening, but her face was set hard as she continued implacably on: "Can't hardly do much a nothin, but she has a common sort of prettiness. So she took up whorin so's to get money for coal and food, so she and her little brother don't freeze or starve to death. And... well, she just hated every minute of it."

There was a dead silence.

"I gotta go," said Sara. And she got up and rushed away.

Next day when Sara came to see Jimmy, she wouldn't look at Hannah. But when Hannah came up to her by the bedside and stroked her hair, she turned and buried her face in the older woman's shoulder.

"Don't you worry," Hannah murmured into her ear. "I made sure that boy won't ever say such a thing to you again."

Bill Wynn made a small sled with a cushioned seat, like a miniature sleigh, so Sara could haul Jonah around more easily, and the Sunday dinners became a weekly event. Elly wasn't sure what Hannah said to Zachary Crabbe, but he never spoke to Sara again. In fact he seemed to spend the entire meal staring at his plate—though he would lift his homely face at odd moments to flash her looks full of both longing and resentment.

By late February, Jimmy was able to get shakily up and come downstairs to join them, and in March he made it to Crapper Jack's. But he was still pale and thin, and all the women fussed over him while Sara looked on indulgently.

Once Jimmy had asked Elly if she had managed to run the purple-necked man to ground as she had promised.

She froze for a moment—then nodded.

"Well then, did yer talk to him? Ask him bout all that business with Harry Orchard and such?"

Elly avoided his eye. "No," she finally said.

"Well why in blazes not?"

"Because somebody shot him first."

Jimmy gaped at her. "Shot him?"

She nodded.

"Dead?"

Another nod.

"Well, who?"

Elly shook her head with a pained expression.

Jimmy stared hard at her. "Well, whose house was that, that big affair up on the hill?"

"It belongs to Charlie Tutt."

"Tutt," said Jimmy. "Feller what owns the Vindicator."

Elly nodded. She watched him put it all together.

"Huh," he finally said. "Well, with that purple-necked feller dead an all, we can't prove nothin, can we? I mean, that's the end of it, ain't it?"

Elly nodded with relief. And hoped that it was.

Toward the end of April the sun stayed out for several days straight. The snow on the streets melted and turned them to mud, which froze each night. Sleighs were put away, buggies and wagons reappeared and made their way between the snow drifts on both sides of the roads. And one bright, unseasonably warm day, the huge double door of Smithson's Machine Shop swung open, and Elly and Lucas pushed the newly-rebuilt Model T Roadster outside for a test drive.

In taking the car apart, they had found the damage to be even more extensive than Lucas had suspected, and the list of parts needing replacement grew each day until Mr. Smithson joked they might as well just go ahead and buy a whole new automobile. But he sent in the orders, boxes full of shiny new parts arrived, and Lucas and Elly spend many blissful hours reassembling the vehicle from the piles of gears and pistons and springs it had become. Lucas once cryptically remarked how "lucky" they were, and Elly caught his meaning at once. It allowed them to probe and understand every element of Henry Ford's ingeniously engineered creation: the planetary gears, revolving around one another like a miniature solar system; detachable head ("makes valve jobs a cinch" marveled Lucas); the vanadium alloy that made the axles and crankshaft so strong. Together they savored each new revelation, Lucas peering sideways at Elly with his funny half-smile. And the day they settled the new crankshaft into its precisely engineered nest inside the engine block, Elly knew how Dr. Frankenstein must have felt when he placed a heart inside the chest of his monster.

By the time it was all reassembled, Elly felt an intimate connection with every nut and bolt of the wonderful machine, and ached with impatience to see it run. They had fired up the engine once inside the shop, Lucas giving her a lesson in how to do it. Now he watched as she adjusted the timing lever on the steering column to retard the spark (so the engine wouldn't kick while starting), jumped out of the cab (the little vehicle had no doors), inserted the crank into a hole beneath the radiator while pulling the wire that operated the choke, then slowly rotated the crank to prime the engine. Finally, pushing the handle with the heel of her hand (Lucas had casually remarked that, if you grabbed a hold of it and it happened to kick back, it could break your wrist), she gave an energetic shove.

The engine fired up with a rattle and a bang.

Elly and Lucas flashed identically subtle smiles at one another.

They climbed in and donned caps and goggles. Elly played with the timing lever until the engine sounded smooth; she glanced at Lucas and he nodded. There were three pedals, working in complicated tandem to control the three gears—two forward, one reverse. But she already understood them so well it was like they were a part of her. Without hesitation she released the handbrake, and—one hand on the throttle—pushed the pedal on the left, engaging the first forward gear.

They began rolling forward.

She grasped the steering wheel and maneuvered them out onto the main road out of town. As they swung out onto the road, they narrowly missed a man on horseback, who cursed at them as they rattled by. The little vehicle bumped and careened over the rutted track. She made the transition from first to second gear, and risked a glance at Lucas. His bone-white hair spilled untidily from his cap; with his pale skin and goggles he looked not quite human. He reached over and pushed the throttle farther in. The plucky little vehicle bucked and tossed, every rut of the road jerking Elly's arms around. They barreled past a dray, spooking a team of horses. Lucas's mouth had taken on the shape it made when he uttered his peculiar laugh, but the engine was making far too much noise for Elly to hear him. The cold wind burned her face, her hair streamed behind her and whipped around her goggles, and she wanted to scream from pure delight.

Suddenly they heard a new, rumbling sound, and realized one of the interurban trains was slowly overtaking them on the track that ran beside the road. They looked at one another again, locking eyes—a rare occurrence—and Elly throttled all the way up. Slowly they began to pull ahead of the train. Lucas flashed Elly the closest thing to a real smile she had ever seen on his expressionless face. From what he had told her, she guessed they were going at least forty-five miles an hour—

BANG! The little car jumped and bucked like a frightened rabbit, skittering all over the road. At the exact same instant, Elly felt the most peculiar sensation, a hot melting of her insides, something damp...

Lucas reached over to pull the brake lever, and they hobbled to a stop beside a snow drift. "Blow out," he remarked cheerfully.

Elly unbuttoned her coat and pulled it aside. A red stain was blooming in the crotch of her overalls.

Lucas glanced at her—then looked quickly away.

"You need," he said in a funny, strained voice, "you need to talk to Hannah."

~~~

She found Hannah dragging a box of coal into the kitchen. Feeling terribly embarrassed and confused, she showed her the stain.

"Oh Lord, Elly," said Hannah, standing up with a hand on her hip and sighing, "is this your first time?"

Elly stared dumbly back at her, more confused than ever. Martha, peeling potatoes at the counter, began to snicker.

Hannah smacked herself in the face. "Nobody's told you a thing, have they?"

Elly shook her head. Martha tittered, and Hannah rolled her eyes.

Hannah assembled a bowl of warm water and a pile of clean rags and, leading Elly to her room, helped her clean herself up. As she worked she asked questions, which quickly revealed the depths of Elly's ignorance.

Then it was back to the kitchen, where Hannah told Martha to "go do something else." Martha sashayed away, smirking over her shoulder. Hannah brewed a pot of tea and joined Elly at the kitchen table. For a few minutes they sat sipping their tea in silence. Finally Hannah cast her eyes heavenward, murmured, "Lord, here we go," then turned to Elly with a bright, matter-of-fact expression.

"So, Elly—have you ever seen a bull mount a cow?"

Elly nodded.

"Well, all right then…"

~~~

Afterward, Elly's primary emotion—once the shock had worn off—was irritation with herself for not having figured out something so mechanically obvious.

• • •

A few days later Elly had already left for the machine shop and Jimmy was alone in the kitchen drinking his morning coffee when Hannah came back from the market bursting with news.

"Well!" she exclaimed. "Jimmy, do you remember that big ship Harold was reading us the article about, one they call the *Titanic*, about to leave on its maiden voyage?"

"Sure, I 'member," said Jimmy. "Biggest in the world."

"Well! Reports are coming in over the telegraph of a terrible disaster of some sort—"

"Did it sink, or what?" asked Jimmy.

"That's what they're saying—but it's still early reports yet, nobody knows much of anything for sure. The whole town is buzzing with it. Big crowd outside the telegraph office, they're posting reports as they come in—"

Three minutes later Jimmy was out the door.

~~~

The crowd outside the telegraph office spilled out into the street. Jimmy jostled his way forward and ran into Pinky.

"Hell with minin," Pinky said genially. "Couldn't miss this."

"So did it sink, or what?" asked Jimmy, breathless.

"Sank like a stone," said a lanky, bearded man standing next to them. "Not enough lifeboats, they're sayin. Be hell to pay, that's sure."

"Holy jumpin turnips!" said Jimmy, thrilled.

"Struck a iceberg, it did," said Pinky.

"A iceberg," marveled Jimmy. "How many killt—they say?"

"Don't know yet," said the man. "Hundreds, that's sure. Should be another report pretty soon, been comin bout every twenty minutes—there, here it comes now!"

Beyond the heads of the people in front of him, Jimmy could see a man removing the chalkboard from the window and replacing it with another. The crowd surged forward. Those in front yelled the news for the benefit of those behind them. Which Jimmy appreciated, since he couldn't read.

"Ship fired distress rockets!" someone bawled. "Ignored by another passing ship!"

"Well that's a rum deal," said Pinky. "Captain oughter be horse-whipped."

"*Flogged*—that's what they call it when you're at sea," said the other man, whom Jimmy had already pegged for a know-it-all. "Be hell to pay, that's sure."

The reports continued to dribble in, but most of them contained little new information. The old Mexican who sold hot tamales had set up his cart nearby. Jimmy bought tamales for himself and Pinky.

"So, when you gonna get yourself hitched to Sara?" Pinky asked him. His merry old eyes twinkled.

Jimmy colored. "Don't know," he mumbled. "Maybe someday."

"Fella could do a lot worse," said Pinky. "She's a plucky one."

"Well," said Jimmy, "I guess she oughter be. Only watched her pa get shot in the head right in front of her."

Pinky's eyebrows shot up.

"When she was just a kid. Got her all toughed up, I 'spect."

"Well I guess it would," agreed Pinky. "How'd her pa come to get shot?"

Jimmy took a bite of his tamale. "It was all on account a Sara saw some feller talkin to that ol Harry Orchard feller," he said, chewing. "Some feller worked for Charlie Tutt. She told her pa, and they killt him for it."

Pinky stared at him. "You don't say."

Jimmy had been been unable to resist a chance to brag on Sara. But now it suddenly occurred to him he might have said too much. "Hey now," he added, "don't you go flappin yer gums about it to no one."

"Sure sure—mum's the word."

"I mean it was just before that train depot got blowed up. So I guess folks still might get stirred up, they knew Tutt was behind it."

Another chalkboard had gone up and people were yelling again. Jimmy ate the last of his tamale and pushed his way back toward the front of the crowd.

Pinky watched his retreating back, nodding to himself. "Well I guess they might," he said softly.

•   •   •

That same afternoon, Mr. Smithson was leaning back in the chair in the office of his machine shop with his feet up on the desk munching on an apple, when he suddenly noticed Elly standing there, Lucas behind her.

"Well hey ya Elly, Lucas. What's cookin?"

"How much," said Elly, "how much for the Model T?"

"The Roadster? Why? You know someone wants to buy it?"

She nodded.

Smithson leaned back even farther and stared at the ceiling, pondering.

"Well let's see. Retail about six-fifty. And the way you two got er fixed up, I 'spect she's about good as new—hell, maybe better!" He chuckled. "And autos bein scarce up here, they go for more. Yep, I 'spect I might get full retail price for it. So," he concluded, "who wants to buy er?"

Elly thrust her hand beneath the bib of her overalls and pulled out a roll of bills.

"Me."

From behind her came a peculiar snuffling sound.

Pinky and five other miners were having lunch. They'd been drilling in the ninth level of the Kentucky Belle, and the air smelt of dust and dynamite. They sat around an overturned metal tub doing duty as a dining table and pulled sandwiches wrapped in waxed paper and flasks of cold tea out of their lunch pails. The lights on their helmets made the shadows around them dance as they chewed and talked.

The conversation, as it had been for the last few days, was of the *Titanic*. Every day brought some new piece of news to kick around. The manager of the White Star Line had told the British papers that the ship was unsinkable, hours after it had already sunk—fodder for an entire lunch hour of jeers and jests. And yesterday they had spent the time working out how to retrieve the five million dollars in diamonds and bonds entombed within the ship on the ocean's floor, with a stand-off between those who thought a diving bell would do the job, those who scoffed that the ocean was too deep, and one man who swore the ship would be nothing but a pile of debris.

Today Ned Bailey had pulled out a newspaper and read aloud about the special train that had been organized for the survivors by the New Haven Railroad. But it seemed they might finally have squeezed the *Titanic* dry, for after a bit of speculation about the scene at the depot when the survivors were embraced by tearful relatives, the conversation languished.

Pinky broke the silence. "Say, talking about that depot reminds me. You may not believe this—but there's new evidence that it weren't the Federation behind Harry Orchard when he blew up the Independence Depot."

"Aw, everyone's heard that old story," scoffed Ned, refilling his pipe.

"Yeah, folks been sayin such-like for years," agreed another. "Ain't never been proved."

"That's just it," said Pinky. "There's a girl *can* prove it."

"A girl? What girl?"

"One of the dancers at Crapper Jack's. Overheard one of Charlie Tutt's men givin Orchard his marchin orders, just before the explosion. She was just a kid. Told her daddy—and they killed him for it."

A miner whistled.

"I always did hear there was a witness got killed," mused Ned.

"Well, that's just it," said Pinky. "They killed the wrong person. It was the girl that heard it all."

They all agreed it was a "hell of a story."

By the end of the day, everyone in the mine knew it.

By the end of the week...

•   •   •

Elly was in the middle of a waltz when she heard the rhythmic thump and swish of dancers' feet grow suddenly ragged and disorganized. She looked out at the room, expecting from long experience to find a fight in progress. But it was the entrance of a group of men that was causing the disturbance.

She brought the song to a finish to a smattering of applause. Crapper Jack had come from behind the bar and was personally escorting the group to a table. It was something she'd never seen him do, and she saw at once that his attention—indeed the attention of the entire room—was focused on a portly man wearing an elegantly-cut suit. Sporting a thick mustache on a broad, meaty, and many-chinned face, he reminded Elly of a butcher dressed for a wedding. The men with him were similarly well-dressed, but had the blunt faces and beefy builds of body guards. Stationed by the door was a man in a green uniform and cap—a man whose open Irish face she recognized. Through the saloon's window she could make out the gleaming forest-green snout of the Pierce-Arrow.

She looked for Sara. She was standing next to Jimmy, both of them taking in the scene. From their casual, curious expressions, it was clear they didn't know yet.

The bartender approached the table with a bottle of Jack's best whiskey and began pouring drinks. The fat man pulled out a cigar. Before he got it to his lips, the man next to him had a gold lighter out. The fat man puffed on his cigar for a moment, then took a sip of whiskey. Jack was making frantic signals for Elly to play again. She was just lifting her hands when the clinking of a spoon on a glass made her pause. Now Jack's frantic signals were for her to be silent.

The fat man rose from his chair.

"I got somethin to say."

The room had already been subdued. Now it went dead silent.

"For those of you don't know, I'm Charlie Tutt. I own the Vindicator, the Excelsior and—oh, a few other things."

He grinned to show what a colossal understatement this was. Dutiful chuckling from the men at his table. Elly saw Sara move close to Jimmy. He squeezed her waist protectively.

Tutt puffed on his cigar, examined it meditatively, then continued:

"Now, there's been some crazy talk of late that one of the girls in this establishment can tie me to Harry Orchard and his heinous crimes. Well, right here and now, I dare this young lady to come forward and repeat this accusation to my face."

He scanned the room. People shifted uncomfortably. Sara had gone rigid, her face pale as death.

"No takers?" said Tutt at last. "Thought as much. And I'll tell you why: this here story—it's nothin but a *damned lie!*"

He paused, puffing on his cigar and glaring around the room. With a sudden chill, Elly realized the chauffeur was staring across the room at her. But his expression was merely quizzical.

"Well," Tutt concluded, "that's all I got to say. Except this young lady would best keep her trap shut from now on. Oh yeah, and one more thing—drinks are on me!"

There was a cheer as men rushed to the bar to take him up on it. Tutt nodded at his men—abruptly they all stood up. He paused for a word with Jack, then swept out the door like an emperor, trailing his men behind him.

On Elly's next break, she and Jimmy and Sara all sat together.

"I'll kill him," said Jimmy, stone-faced. "Swear to Christ I will."

"Jimmy Jimmy, you promised me," said Sara, squeezing his shoulder. "You promised you'd just let it be."

Jimmy sat rigidly, refusing to meet her eyes. Sara stared helplessly at Elly. Elly thought for a while, then spoke.

"All the mine owners might be involved."

Jimmy didn't seem to be listening.

"If you kill Tutt," she continued in her toneless voice, "you take a chance they'll find out it was you."

Finally Jimmy turned and looked at her.

"And that would lead them straight to Sara."

They stared each other down—then Jimmy seemed to deflate like a pricked balloon.

"All right," he said.

News of Tutt's speech quickly spread over the whole valley, and the next evening the dinner table at Hannah Moffet's boarding house was abuzz with speculation.

"Hit's suspicious, that's what it is," opined Harold Baxter. "I mean, why's 'e making such a big stink if 'e ain't worried about sumping?"

Zachary Crabbe, who worked in one of Tutt's mines, mumbled that Tutt "ain't so bad, least he don't hire no dagoes"—before noticing how Bill Wynn's mild blue eyes were fixed on him, and relapsing into his usual mute condition. While Pinky, who would normally be spouting all manner of rumors and opinions, was staring at his plate, strangely silent. Jimmy watched him throughout the meal, and cornered him in the parlor after it was finished.

"Hey—was it *you* went all round yappin bout what Sara seen?"

"What, me?" Pinky's eyes opened wide. "Not a word."

"Well keep it that way. If her name gets out…"

"Ain't nobody knows which girl it was," said Pinky confidently.

Jimmy stared hard at him. "Why you so sure?"

Pinky blushed.

"Jus remember what I said," said Jimmy, walking away—and bumping into Zachary Crabbe on the other side of the doorway. Jimmy gave him a suspicious look and he scuttled away.

Several weeks later everything had died down.

A slender girl driving a smart little automobile was now a familiar sight on the streets of Cripple Creek. She sported a man's cap and goggles, let her long black hair blow in the wind, and seemed to delight in honking her horn at anything in her way. She could be seen not just in the town, but tearing around the whole valley. Sometimes she was alone, sometimes a pale-haired boy took turns at the wheel. And sometimes there were three passengers: a young man in the passenger seat with a pretty fair-haired girl on his lap—and in the tiny seat above the trunk, a small boy sitting high above the road, waving to everybody they passed and looking as though he might die of happiness.

By late May the wildflowers were starting to bloom, dusting the barren hills surrounding the town with pastel colors, and the air had a freshness that went to your head. Perhaps that's what made Elly break her long-standing habit of never mentioning her birthday. Even Jimmy had no idea when it was (since he didn't know his own, it had never occurred to him to ask). But as Elly and Lucas sat together in the sun, taking a break from Elly's welding lesson (she was finally getting the hang of it), she broke their usual comfortable silence to announce:

"Today I turned thirteen."

Lucas puffed on his cigarette and nodded dreamily, as though savoring the information and tobacco in equal measure, but said nothing.

Next day they were cleaning up when Lucas offhandedly pointed to something in the corner. Elly went to investigate, and found a roll of canvas tied up with attached canvas laces. She untied and unrolled it—and found, nestled in pockets sewn into the canvas, a set of gleaming wrenches in graduated sizes.

"Drop forged," murmured Lucas.

It was the first birthday present Elly had received in the last seven years, and it brought hot tears to her eyes. She carefully rolled up the beautiful tools and walked over to Lucas. They stood very close and looked directly into one another's eyes for a long moment; Elly could almost feel his heart beating in the air between them.

"Thank you," she said.

Lucas nodded.

Then his eyes shifted and he walked away.

Next morning it was another perfect day—perhaps the day, Elly thought, she would leave the valley and try the road to Colorado Springs, a steep, winding wagon trail that, since the trains had been built, was poorly maintained. She had even heard that parts of it had been washed away in the spring run-off.

It sounded to Elly like a perfect adventure.

She was just checking everything—oil, tire pressure, fuel level—when she suddenly noticed that a figure that had alighted from the streetcar in the distance, and was running jerkily toward her.

With a shock, she realized it was Bill Wynn.

"Elly, Elly!" he shouted as he rushed up. His eyes were wild. He pulled off his hat and ran his fingers through his thin hair distractedly. "Elly, where's Hannah?"

Elly was so amazed to see the usually placid Bill in such a state, she could hardly respond. By the time she pointed to the house, he was already dashing up the porch steps in huge bounds, calling Hannah's name. A minute later he was back, pulling Hannah—still in her apron—by the hand. Hannah looked terrified.

"Bill, what is it? What's happened? Oh Lord, Bill, was anybody killed?"

Bill took no notice of her. Still wild-eyed, he asked Elly if she could drive them over to the Cresson. She nodded and fired up the Roadster. Bill climbed into the passenger seat and pulled Hannah onto his lap. Elly got in and donned cap and goggles. Hannah was still plying Bill with questions, none of which he would answer, saying only, "You'll see, you'll see..."

They motored off. Elly decided Bill's manner warranted a full throttle, and the little car flew along the gravelly track. Stones thumped and banged against the undercarriage. Hannah had given up and sat mute, her face a mask of apprehension. While Bill looked—whenever Elly glanced over at him—completely mad.

They arrived at the road leading up to the mine entrance. Elly geared down and they ascended the winding track. When they reached the top, the same man she remembered from before rushed toward them. Beneath his battered fedora, his face held the same look of near-hysteria as Bill's, and Elly was certain there had been some awful calamity.

"How's everything, George?"

"Harold's got er all under control, Mr. Vin," said George, tipping his hat and ushering them into the little building where the lift sat waiting. And now Elly noticed something in George's manner that gave her pause: could the man be actually suppressing a grin?

"Bill, Bill," cried Hannah, perhaps sensing the same thing. "Oh Lord Bill, what's happened?"

"George," said Bill, "you got any more of those magnesium flares?"

"Got some right here, sure Mr. Vin," said George, handing him some. Helmets were strapped onto Hannah and Elly, their lamps lit, and a moment later they were descending the mine shaft.

"Nothing to worry about this time, Elly," said Bill, squeezing her waist. "Won't be any blasting today. In fact, there may not be any blasting for a very long time."

He began to giggle in a most alarming manner.

"Bill now—I just can't stand it!" cried Hannah, beating him on the shoulder. "Bill, you've got to tell—"

"Hannah, Elly," said Bill, pulling them both close. "You know how I'm always saying, 'Well, one of these days'?"

Elly looked up at Bill. The light from her helmet illuminated a face that might have been lit from within by sheer joy.

"Oh Lord, Bill—you don't mean—?"

"Hannah—today's the day!"

~~~

They stopped at a level deep within the mine and started down a tunnel. A short time later they saw lights in the distance, and came upon a large group of miners standing near a ladder leaning against the side of the tunnel. Sparks flew from some welding going on nearby.

The sight of Bill set the men whooping.

"It's Bill!"

"Lucky Bill! That's what we a-call him from-a now on! Lucky Bill!"

Manic laughter. Harold Baxter came up to them with a smile that showed every one of his spectacularly crooked teeth. "Hannah, Elly—well, hain't we got a show for em, Gov'ner!"

"How's the door coming, Harold?"

"We'll 'ave er in place in three shakes. Wouldn't do to leave Aladdin's Cave open to the public—hit's a high-grader's paradise, something like!"

"Aladdin's Cave?" repeated Hannah wonderingly. The men all chuckled madly; everything seemed funny to them, thought Elly.

"Hannah, Hannah," said Bill, catching his breath. "Here boys, let her get a look."

They cleared away from the base of the ladder. Bill paused to light one of the flares. When Elly's eyes had adjusted to its blinding light, she saw there was a hole in the side of the tunnel, about ten feet up. Hannah climbed up, Bill behind her with the flare. She peered into the hole—and let out a shriek. Which got the men all chuckling again and slapping each other's backs.

"Oh just wait till you see er, Elly," said Harold. "It's called a vug—a big hole full of crystals. Like a geode, only giant, like. Biggest one anyone's ever heard of. And the crystals—well, every one of em's *chock full of bleedin gold!*"

Hannah was descending the ladder, speechless, her face radiant.

Bill helped Elly onto the ladder and followed behind with the flare as she climbed to the top. At first she could hardly see, the sight was so dazzling. When her eyes finally adjusted, she realized she was looking inside a high, narrow cavern some forty feet tall and twenty feet wide—and the light was so dazzling because the entire thing was lined from floor to ceiling with crystals. In the flare's bright light they shone with the brilliance of a thousand tiny suns. She examined a few, growing mushroom-like from the walls beside her, and saw they were made of milky white quartz veined with gold. Flakes of gold the size of her thumbnail were scattered like confetti on the floor beneath them.

She feasted on the enchanted vision until her flare finally sputtered out, then clambered back down. The miners had gone strangely quiet, and she saw they were all staring at something with broad grins. She followed their eyes—and blushed to the roots of her hair.

Bill and Hannah were locked together in a kiss, the likes of which Elly had only read—or dreamt—about.

Chapter Nine

Surprises

Overnight Bill Wynn had become rich beyond anything he ever dreamt of, and he found the sudden change in his fortune "pretty discombobulating." Worst of all, for a man so naturally trusting, were the extreme precautions he was forced to take. For even though he paid his miners huge bonuses (and the highest wages anyone had ever heard of), the temptation to "high-grade"—sneak out the fantastically rich ore—was overwhelming. He was forced to have everyone searched, and the steel door to "Aladdin's's Cave"—to which only he and Harold Baxter had keys—had to have armed guards posted before it day and night.

The gold mounted up at an alarming rate, for the crystals were so loaded with the stuff they needed almost no refining. "A child with a hammer could extract it," Bill marveled. Banks lined up, eager to advance him any amount of money. So it was only a few days after the strike that Bill sat down at the kitchen table with Elly to transact some business, while Hannah looked on.

"Well now, Elly. Here's the agreement we signed for that loan you fronted me. Let's see," said Bill, scanning the document, "eighteen hundred dollars, twenty percent interest…tell you what I'm gonna do."

He held up the paper and, grinning, ripped it in half.

Elly blinked at him. Hannah covered her mouth to stifle a laugh.

"What say we up the interest a bit? To, say—a thousand percent? That would be eighteen thousand dollars, add the principal that makes nineteen thousand eight hundred. Say we call it an even twenty thousand."

He pulled a huge stack of bills from a paper bag and laid them in front of Elly. She stared at the money, unable to keep from running calculations in her mind: twenty thousand dollars would buy an enormous house. Four Pierce-Arrows. A fleet of Model T Roadsters...

Bill was holding out his hand to her. "What say, Elly? We square?"

Elly's eyes gleamed, and they shook on it.

On the following day, Elly and Lucas set off together in the Roadster on the road to Colorado Springs. With Lucas's guidance, she had equipped her automobile with a full set of tools and essential spare parts, as well as a gasoline can, a shovel, and coil of rope. All of this was stored in a metal box welded to the rear, for they had turned the trunk into a small upholstered seat so Sara could sit in the back with Jonah. While Lucas had come up with an invention all his own: a small mirror mounted above the windshield so the driver could see backward. (Since Elly was always the fastest thing on the road, she wondered when she would ever need it; Lucas smiled his enigmatic smile, but said nothing.)

They left mid-morning with a bag of sandwiches and a supply of coffee, kept hot in an ingenious new kind of insulated container called a "thermos." After climbing the rim of the valley, they immediately found themselves on a series of descending switchbacks. The slope was so steep they looked over the tops of the trees, and the narrow rutted track was as ill-maintained as Elly had heard; it took all her skill to keep the little vehicle from pitching over the side.

From time to time she glanced at Lucas. He looked serenely back at her.

At the foot of the mountain the road disappeared into a creek, emerging on the far bank. She stopped the car. The creek was swift-moving and swollen with spring snowmelt. Lucas got out, removed his shoes and stockings, rolled up his trousers and waded in. He moved carefully, testing each step and leaning against the current to avoid being swept away. In the middle, the water foamed against his thighs. He waded back. His feet were blue with cold. He replaced shoes and stockings and climbed back in the Roadster. Elly looked a question at him, and he shrugged. But she saw the look of sly challenge in his goggled eyes, returned it with a look of her own—and plunged the Roadster into the stream. Before they reached the middle, water was pouring over the doorless sides of the cab, and they both lifted their feet as it swirled over the floor. But the little automobile plowed steadily on and emerged onto the far bank, dripping water like a wet horse.

They continued on. The road ascended another series of switchbacks, through forests of sun-dappled pines and aspen, and then they were hugging the side of an almost vertical mountain, descending at a steady rate. Far across the gorge a train threaded in and out of a tunnel on its way to Cripple Creek. Lucas had her put the car into low gear to slow it down and save the brakes. The drop over the side was so steep that if Elly had leapt out of the car's open side there might have been enough time for most of her brief life to flash through her mind's eye before it abruptly ended.

She concentrated on the ruined track, anticipating each loose stone or jagged rut. Her arms and back ached as she fought to control the wheel. From time to time a stream cascaded from above and cut a gash of erosion through the road, and she would race across to avoid getting stuck. Where an avalanche of loose earth blocked the road they took turns with the shovel until there was enough room to skirt the edge.

Finally they descended into a valley. The road leveled out, and they sped across a dry, dusty plain studded with enormous, curiously-shaped sandstone boulders, like full-sized sand castles half washed away by an incoming tide. At the base of one of them a road branched off, ascending the mountain beside them at an impossibly steep angle to what looked like the entrance of a mine.

They looked at one another, and silently agreed it was a challenge they couldn't resist.

The angle *was* impossible, and halfway up, the engine balked and stalled. Elly thought she would have to back down with her foot on the brake, but Lucas murmured: "Try it in reverse."

At once Elly understood. For it was a curious fact that reverse gear on the Roadster was geared even lower than first. She backed down to a spot wide enough to swerve perpendicular to the road, got out and restarted the engine—and they began crawling up the hill backwards. Elly twisted her head to see the road, heard the snuffling sound of Lucas's laughter—and realized he was pointing at the little mirror he had mounted above the windshield; with a little practice, she found she could use it to steer by.

The road indeed terminated at an old abandoned mine. But the entrance was blocked by broken and rotting timbers, like a mouth full of ruined teeth. Without discussing it, they removed their goggles and set off, carrying the coffee and sandwiches, to climb the short distance to the top of the mountain. From its windy summit they could dimly make out the distant city of Colorado Springs. The colossal outline of Pikes Peak challenged the brilliant blue sky.

The moment was utterly perfect. They looked directly into one another's eyes for a long instant...

Then they got out the sandwiches.

"Holy jumpin turnips, Elly—you sure about this?"

Elly nodded. She and Jimmy had always split whatever money came their way fifty-fifty, and she didn't see why this should be any different.

Jimmy turned the stack of bills over and over in his hands. "Can't hardly...what I mean to say is... My mouth jus done dried up with words now, it has." He raised his eyes from the money to Elly. "We's really partners, ain't we Elly? Straight down the line."

Elly nodded again. Jimmy reached out and ruffled her hair. Then a sudden thought lit up his face, and he grinned conspiratorially.

"Hey, all this money...well there's somethin I been savin up to do, and now..."

He began explaining, and Elly nodded enthusiastic approval. It took them two weeks to accomplish. Two weeks in which they could be seen motoring all over town on mysterious errands, the Roadster loaded down with packages and crates from the depot. They made one last check that everything was ready, then drove up the rutted track of Poverty Gulch. Before Elly even had the engine shut off, Sara was standing at the door of her shack with her arms crossed.

"Finally decided to come round, huh? I thought you just forgot all about us."

"Ain't forgot," said Jimmy cheerfully, bounding from the Roadster and leaping across the ditch. "Been busy."

"Yeah? Well there's a boy in there thinks you did." She glanced at Elly, including her in her scorn.

"Jimmy, Jimmy is that you?" came Jonah's voice.

"Yeah, it's me Jonah!" Jimmy uncrossed Sara's arms and grasped her hands, grinning strangely at her.

"What?" she said.

"Jimmy," cried Jonah, "Jimmy, can I go for a ride?"

"Well now," said Jimmy, leading Sara inside, the same irrepressible grin on his face, "what's happenin here is, we's all goin for a ride—an ain't never comin back!"

Sara stared at him.

"What I mean to say is, y'all's movin away from this place."

"Movin? Movin where?"

"Somewheres else."

"When? When are we movin, Jimmy?" said Jonah, sitting up in bed, excited.

"Well," said Jimmy, letting go of one of Sara's hands to rub his chin reflectively, "seems to me the best time would be—RIGHT NOW!"

Sara's eyes popped. She glanced at Elly, and knew her well enough to detect the sly look in her eyes. "Y'all are *crazy*!" she sputtered.

"Now come on," said Jimmy, ignoring her, suddenly energized. "No time to waste! Yez leavin this place right this minute, once an for all!"

"We's leavin, Sary!" cried Jonah, bouncing on the mattress. "Ain't never comin back!"

"What are y'all *talkin* about!" wailed Sara, now genuinely alarmed. "I can't leave without things for cookin—"

"Don't need em," said Jimmy.

"Don't need—? But clothes, our clothes—"

"Don't need them neither. Jus grab a few things, throw em in the ol Roadster, and let's jus GIT!"

"Let's just GIT, Sary!" cried Jonah, gleeful.

"Oh Jesus wept and Moses crept," muttered Sara. She began running around distractedly, gathering armloads of clothing and miscellaneous belongings and stuffing them into whatever was at hand—laundry basket, washtub—and passing them to Jimmy and Elly, who ferried them to the Roadster and tied everything down.

"That's it, that's all she'll take," said Jimmy. "Now it's time to GIT!"

"Oh!" wailed Sara—they were all in a sort of giddy hysteria now. "Wait, the tintype of my folks!" She snatched it from the wall. "And, and the bible—"

She grabbed it, Jimmy grabbed Jonah, and they all trooped to the Roadster. The back was so full that Sara had to sit on Jimmy's lap, Jonah atop both of them. Elly cranked the engine and they rattled off in the overloaded vehicle, teetering precariously. Jonah was laughing, and Sara looked stunned. Down Poverty Gulch, right on Main, then left on a small side street lined with modest frame houses. And at one of these—a neat little cottage with frilly blue curtains—they came to a stop.

"What in the—?" said Sara.

They got out. Jimmy carried Jonah and led them to the front door. He nodded at Elly, and she pulled a key from her pocket and put it in Sara's hand.

"Well go on," said Jimmy. "Open er up!"

Sara mutely obeyed, and the door swung open. She stood at the threshold, gaping.

The parlor was furnished with a rug, sofa, arm chairs, side tables, and lamps, everything looking brand new. Sara gave an inarticulate cry, glanced at Jimmy—then rushed through the room and into the kitchen, the rest following behind. An enameled coal stove and gleaming oak ice box, shiny pots and pans hanging on the walls, matching china dishes stacked neatly on the counter. Sara began laughing, clutched at Jimmy, then led them into the dining room. She ran her hands over a maple table and sideboard, exclaimed at a vase full of fresh flowers, then continued into a hallway leading to two bedrooms. In the first, an array of pretty dresses filled an open wardrobe (and now she remembered how Elly had casually asked her dress size). And in the second bedroom (in addition to a selection of games and puzzles, a toy battleship, and a dresser full of neatly-folded boy's clothing), stood a small wicker chair with shiny metal wheels.

"Is it for me?" cried Jonah, squirming in Jimmy's arms. A moment later he was tearing up and down the hallway, whooping "Look at me, Sary! Look at me!"

But Sara couldn't look, because she and Jimmy were busy with a kiss so expert that Elly wondered if Bill and Hannah hadn't given them pointers. When they finally broke away, both of them red-faced and grinning, Jimmy whispered something in Sara's ear.

"Well of course I will, you fool!" she cried, her face radiant.

And she kissed him again.

• • •

It was decided there would be a double wedding.

That Hannah would allow herself to be married beside a girl who had been one of Crapper Jack's whores set the tongues of the town's busy-bodies wagging. But Hannah had developed a fierce, almost maternal affection for the younger woman, ignored their primly poisonous gibes, and stood firm.

Hannah had been waiting four years and was not disposed to wait much longer. This suited Sara and Jimmy just fine, and they set the date for the first of July. This would give the miners in Hannah's boarding house time to find new lodgings, while Bill and Hannah searched for a home befitting their new station. They had decided they would not move to Colorado Springs like the other millionaires (which it was quite clear Bill would soon be) but stay in Cripple Creek. Bill found himself hard-pressed, though, to get Hannah to adapt to her new status as a "lady of leisure"; it was all he could do get her to hire a woman to help cook and clean to the end of the month. And Hannah still insisted on baking her own pies and cakes.

During her year in Cripple Creek, Elly's playing had progressed wonderfully. She had grown taller, and discovered a way of using her long slender arms and wrists as though cracking a whip, lending a snapping power and urgency to her rhythms. And her improvising had reached the point where new arabesques and flights of fancy seemed to bloom under her fingers of their own volition. She had only to sit back and lose herself in the colors flashing through her mind…

One night, during the hectic weeks before the wedding, she wrapped up a set with a particularly rambunctious rendition of "Waiting for the Robert E. Lee." It had all the unattached dancers (even Sara!) doing the sassy cakewalk that helped pack Crapper Jack's every night, and the audience's loud applause brought Elly abruptly back to earth. She looked up to find a familiar dapper, derbied, dark-skinned figure beaming at her from the side of the stage.

"Miss Elly, you done took old Sam's breath away, so you did!" cried Sam. He knew Elly well enough to see through her impassive face to the smile in her eyes. It was time for her break, but Sam declined to sit with her for some reason. Instead, he suggested they stroll back to Sam's saloon together, for he was back on the job, taking a break himself. Outside on the street, Elly pointed out her Roadster.

Sam made a face of exaggerated surprise and delight. "And you drives it around all by your lonesome, Miss Elly?"

She nodded proudly.

"Well don't that just take the cake!"

"I can take you for a ride," she suggested.

"Well we surely must do that, yessir we'll do that someday," enthused Sam. "Say"—he deftly changed the subject—"you know that piano of yours could use a little tuning up…"

Before he left for the winter, Sam had been Cripple Creek's most sought-after piano tuner, and Elly looked forward to getting the instrument at Crapper Jack's finally tuned to her satisfaction. She met him there the following afternoon, watched him work for a while, then asked if she could try it.

"Now the most important thing," said Sam, handing her the wrench, "is don't go twisting it back and forth, cause if you do you'll ream her out, and the tuning won't hold. You got to *tap* the handle, real gentle…"

It reminded Elly of making delicate valve adjustments on an engine, and she quickly got the hang of it. While the most difficult part of tuning—finding the pitches—was child's play for Elly with her perfect ear, and within a few minutes she was systematically working her way up the keyboard.

"Well I shoulda known," said Sam, chuckling. "If I had another wrench, I declare you'd be putting poor old Sam out of business!"

Elly stopped tuning and examined the wrench. She turned to Sam with a sly look.

"Can I borrow it for one day?"

Sam agreed, and the following afternoon, she and Lucas created a perfect duplicate. When Sam saw it, he laughed and laughed.

He continued, though, to put off Elly's offer of a ride in her Roadster.

Two weeks before the wedding, Hannah and Sara took the train to Colorado Springs to order their wedding gowns, for Bill insisted there was nothing in Cripple Creek grand enough for Hannah now; it must be one of the expensive shops on Pikes Peak Avenue with all the latest Paris fashions. Hannah had balked, unwilling to hurt her friend Nellie Smeltzer's feelings by not patronizing her dress shop—then hit on the idea of hiring Nellie as a "paid consultant." Martha and Elly were to be bridesmaids, and Moosie would of course be the flower girl, so it was a big, lively, all-female group that set off one glorious June morning on the train.

The wildflowers were out in force, and the aspens sported fresh green foliage of a delicate hue.

"Wouldn't that be a pretty shade of green for a gown!" enthused Hannah.

"Not for a wedding gown," sniffed Nellie Smeltzer.

"We could just wear leaves," suggested Martha. "Like Eve."

This set everyone laughing, and they all began chattering again—that is, everyone but Elly. But they all knew her, and realized she was entirely content to just sit and be the recipient of Moosie's kaleidoscopic observations.

"It's bump bump bumpity on a train," cried the little girl, matching actions to words by bouncing in her seat. "Like, like playing the piano!" she enthused. "And, and then—then you're hungry!"

Outside the windows were the same breathtaking vistas Elly remembered from her recent automobiling adventure. The old wagon trail she and Lucas had driven was visible on the other side of the canyon as a scratch on the flank of a massive granite mountain. They flew across trestles spanning heart-in-your-mouth gorges and shot into tunnels where the train's sound doubled, mixed with ear-piercing screams—for Moosie had decided that screaming was the appropriate response to being in a tunnel. At the end of the last tunnel, the plains of eastern Colorado suddenly appeared, receding in a shimmery haze, a tawny sea with Kansas the far shore.

A short time later, they pulled into the station. Nellie unfurled her parasol and led a twittering procession through the neat, bustling young city, which owed its prosperity to the scrappy mining town from which they had embarked. At once Elly found herself perspiring, for they had descended five thousand feet from fresh spring to hot, dusty summer. She noticed that horse-drawn vehicles shared the wide streets with an almost equal number of automobiles, including several Model T's. But none of them, she noted with satisfaction, were Roadsters.

Nellie led them to an elaborate, high-ceilinged establishment where a neatly-dressed female clerk helped them agonize deliciously over various fabrics and designs. Hannah was still not used to being a rich lady and could not stop herself from remarking on the scandalous prices. Nellie proclaimed that nothing but silk would do for a wedding gown, but allowed Hannah to talk her into a very pale green instead of the ivory Nellie preferred. Finally they were all measured, the gowns were ordered (to be sent to Cripple Creek, where Nellie would do the final alterations), and Hannah peeled off four hundred dollar bills from the roll Bill had given her, trying to act like it was an everyday thing, and not at all succeeding.

Then it was off to luncheon at the magnificent new Antlers Hotel. Nellie took advantage of Hannah's largesse to order fresh oysters, which had been shipped by train from the coast on ice and cost two dollars and thirty-five cents for a dozen. The others watched in fascination as she devoured them raw. Moosie begged to try one and immediately threw up all over the linen tablecloth. But even this couldn't dampen their high spirits, and when they were back on the street, they decided to take in a moving picture show.

Besides the kinetoscope "chasers" of her vaudeville days, Elly had sampled a few of these on her travels with Jimmy. He preferred westerns and she had gone along with him; she had found them fascinating yet trivial, full of cowboys and Indians and horses in constant dizzying motion.

But they were always shown in cheap, tawdry rooms smelling of sweat and tobacco, and the place they entered now was an elaborate theater with plush seats and uniformed attendants. A film was already in progress as they took their seats, a travelogue showing slant-eyed people in exotic dress. This ended shortly and something entitled *What Happened to Mary* came on, an adventure story featuring a pretty, plucky girl menaced by a mustachioed villain. Hannah began reading the title cards for Moosie's benefit—but each title prompted three more questions from Moosie until the people nearby began to hiss at them. Elly was distracted as well by the ineptly-played piano accompaniment, and judged the music poorly coordinated to the action. But the things happening on the screen were quite exciting, and Sara, sitting next to her, gripped Elly's hand. The villain was just about to throw poor bound-and-gagged Mary from a cliff when a final title announced, "To be continued in the next exciting installment!"

"Well, ain't that a kick in the teeth," muttered Sara.

The feature attraction now began. And suddenly, for the first time in her life, Elly realized what a moving picture might be.

It was entitled *The Lonely Villa,* and its plot was both ingenious and exciting. A gang of outlaws make a telephone call to a doctor living in the eponymous villa, calling him away from home on a false alarm, then break into the house. His wife barricades herself in the doctor's office with their young son, then manages to reach her husband with another telephone call and alert him to their plight. He races home by every possible conveyance—at one point even commandeering a gypsy caravan—while the outlaws struggle to break into the barricaded room...

What was wonderful (and a revelation to Elly) was the way the action shifted back and forth between the villains chopping at the door, the wife piling ever more furniture in front of it, and her husband's mad race home. Back and forth, faster and faster—until it became so exciting Elly ceased to care about the inept pianist, Sara dug her fingernails into Elly's palm, and Moosie was rendered mute with amazement.

Then they were all outside, blinking in the bright sunlight. Sara had just the right words for the experience.

"Feels like," she said, shaking her head in wonder, "like we just walked out of a dream."

Elly met often with Sam in the afternoons, for she had neglected her piano practice of late, and he had learned some new tunes to teach her. He always seemed to find some excuse, though, to put off Elly's offer of a ride in the Roadster. But he must have sensed her growing disappointment, for one day he reluctantly gave in.

He sat looking stiff and uncomfortable as they motored through the town. But once they were in the open countryside, he loosened up, leaning back and smiling broadly at the sight of Elly in her cap and goggles expertly maneuvering the little vehicle along the rutted track.

"Well well, Miss Elly, I shoulda known the way you play that piano you'd be just a demon for speed!" he remarked, chuckling.

They were motoring back into town when one of a group of boys lounging by the side of a building pointed at them, exclaimed something to the others—and a moment later the Roadster was being pelted with stones. Elly throttled up while Sam ducked down, clutching his derby. The automobile's side banged hollowly as some of the missiles found their target. They were almost out of range when Sam suddenly let out a groan, and Elly realized he'd been hit.

They rolled to a stop in front of Sam's saloon. Sam was holding a bloody handkerchief to his forehead. Elly stared at him in mute dismay.

"It's all right, Miss Elly, really it is," said Sam, forcing a smile. "This don't even signify to one with as tough a hide as old Sam, no sir. I just hope those hooligans didn't hurt your pretty little automobile." He finished mopping himself and replaced the derby on his head. And Elly was reminded of the time a trio of cowboys had knocked the derby from the head of another colored man named Smiley Hobson, and her six-year-old self had raced into a crowded street to retrieve it.

Sam seemed to read her thoughts, because he reached over and gave her hand a gentle squeeze.

"Just the way the world is, Miss Elly," he said softly. "Complainin about it does about as much good as complainin about the weather. So you just forget all about it, cause old Sam already has. Yessir, only thing old Sam's gonna remember about today is how he had hisself a fine little ride."

He squeezed her hand again and strode away a bit shakily—but with his head erect.

Chapter Ten

Escape

The little Methodist church was full to overflowing with a motley mixture of miners, merchants, Bill Wynn's brother Elks, and dance hall girls from Crapper Jack's in their gaudiest finery. Many of the people were barely known or even complete strangers to Bill and Hannah, for as Bill had wryly remarked, strike it rich and suddenly everybody is your friend. Elly had even talked Lucas into making an appearance, though he and his ill-fitting suit looked equally unhappy with one another. Bill and Jimmy, on the other hand, had made their own excursion to the best tailor in Colorado Springs and were resplendent in striped pants, swallow-tail coats, and high stiff collars.

Jimmy had come downstairs after getting dressed and asked Elly what she thought. She looked at the handsome, elegantly-dressed young man and remembered a boy in ragged clothes whose leather eye patch was held on by a shoelace. She was filled with an emotion new to her: a sense of time's indomitable march; of things lost never to be regained. Jimmy smiled—her look was answer enough. And perhaps he felt something similar at the sight of Elly in her bridesmaid's gown, for his gray eye glistened as he shyly mumbled that she looked "real pretty."

Now the wheezy pump organ was playing the wedding march from *Lohengrin*, and everyone stood and turned to watch the brides walk down the aisle side-by-side. Somehow Hannah's ungainliness had been transformed by the lovely, lace-trimmed silk gown—and by her own radiance—into stateliness. While Sara, Elly decided, was simply beautiful. Moosie trailed behind them carrying a bouquet of freshly-picked daisies, and made a game of pretending to step on this or that flowing train—then impishly refraining at the last minute. Jonah, dressed to the nines, his wheelchair in a place of honor up front, began to giggle—until a look from Sara silenced him.

The ceremony went smoothly, though the murmured "I do's" were, Elly suspected, inaudible to most of the congregation (all but Hannah's, which had a quality of "Well, what do you think!" and caused some titters). Everything happened very fast, and it seemed but a moment later that Martha, with rather unladylike athleticism, managed to catch both thrown bouquets (inspiring one of the dance hall girls to predict she'd be a bigamist).

Then they were filing out of the church, where the elegant carriage Bill had rented stood waiting to transport the brides and grooms to the National Hotel for the reception. Parked directly behind it, to Elly's surprise, was the Pierce-Arrow. The chauffeur was leaning against it, smoking a cigarette. As the wedding party advanced down the church steps, he opened the rear door of the gleaming auto, and Charlie Tutt eased his bulk from the back seat and advanced on Bill with outstretched hand.

"Bill! Congratulations, old man. Just had to stop by and give you my best wishes. And is this the blushing bride?..."

Elly and Lucas wandered together over to the elegant automobile. At the sight of Lucas, the Irish chauffeur's ruddy face lit up.

"Hey, Lucas!" he cried, tossing away his cigarette. "Sure you're just the man I need to see. Started hearin this clinkety-clunk sound on the way over here, seemed to come from behind."

"Differential," murmured Lucas. "Maybe the U-joint."

A moment later Lucas, oblivious of his suit, was crawling underneath the vehicle. The chauffeur pulled a handkerchief from his pocket and tied it around his face to keep off dripping oil, then crawled underneath beside him. Charlie Tutt was still booming on in hail-fellow-well-met style as Bill and Hannah listened politely. Jimmy and Sara stood stiffly off to the side.

Lucas and the chauffeur emerged from underneath the Pierce-Arrow. The chauffeur still had the handkerchief covering the lower half of his face, and Sara happened to glance at him.

Nobody noticed how her face went white.

~~~

The National Hotel was the pride of Cripple Creek, and the equal, everyone said, of Denver's Brown Palace. Bill had told the manager to "lay out a feed trough of nothing but the best, sky's the limit," and the guests descended like a starving horde on a buffet that included roast partridge and quail, as well as lobster and crab ferried in by express train. A mountain of ice cream had been sculpted into the shape of the Cresson mine, and the cake was a seven-tiered affair taller than Moosie. Who stood gazing up at it in awe—before swiping a fingerful of icing.

They had asked Elly to play for the reception. But she had demurred and instead suggested Sam, who had assembled a small colored ensemble of piano, fiddle and banjo.

"They're special black men to play special, special *married* music," Moosie declared.

Elly had somehow ended up in charge of her, and was savoring her idiosyncratic remarks. The band struck up "When It's Springtime in the Rockies," and the newly-married couples began swirling around the room as everyone applauded. Sara had a rather dazed look, which Elly attributed to the shock of finding oneself suddenly married. Jimmy whispered something in her ear and she flashed him a smile, but it still appeared strained. People joined the two dancing couples, and by the next song it seemed everyone was dancing but Elly. Perhaps this was because the women from Crapper Jack's were now available without dance tickets. Even Zachary Crabbe, looking stiff in an equally stiff-looking suit, was being spun around by cross-eyed Iris. Moosie pointed at him.

"Zachary Crabbe dances like, like the Man-in-the-Moon," she pronounced, giggling. "And, and he talks to the man in the green car."

Elly suddenly realized Jimmy was standing before her, Sara at his side.

"Elly," he said, "yer wanner…wanner dance?"

Elly felt herself blushing; in all their years together it was something they had never done. Sara still seemed preoccupied, but managed an encouraging smile. Sam had struck up "And the Band Played On," and Elly allowed herself to be led out onto the dance floor. The feeling that she was somehow losing Jimmy had been growing inside her all day, and now it gripped her. As they danced, Jimmy expertly leading, she had a sudden peculiar desire to press herself against him—a frightening feeling that only intensified when he murmured into her ear that she would always be his "best pal."

The song ended. Jimmy kissed her clumsily on the cheek, gave her a wry smile—and went back to Sara. Elly found herself once again standing beside Moosie and feeling dazed. Then something Moosie had recently said suddenly struck her as funny.

"So," she said to Moosie, "Zachary Crabbe talked to the man in the green car?"

Moosie was as astounded as everyone else whenever Elly spoke unprompted, and stared at her open-mouthed before finally nodding.

"Um-hmm. Talked to the, the big fat man in the, the big fat car."

"Right after the wedding?"

Moosie nodded distractedly, plainly bored, then ran over to see Jonah. Elly looked around the room for Crabbe and spotted him standing in a corner. She tried to think what in the world the shy youth could have to say to a man like Charlie Tutt but could think of only one thing. She looked more closely at him and saw he was watching Sara and Jimmy dance. Watching them the way a cat watches goldfish swimming in a bowl…

She was growing more and more alarmed. Moosie had decided to dance with Jonah by pushing him around the floor in his wheelchair, to his manifest delight. Elly decided to leave off watching her, and shadow Crabbe instead.

She drifted across the room to stand behind him, and was just in time to overhear him ask a group of miners where Sara and Jimmy were staying the night. This provoked a few ribald comments, but no one seemed to know for certain.

A song was ending. Bill and Hannah left the dance floor, and in the short interval before people began to fuss over them again, Crabbe sidled up to them.

"So, ah, Mr. Wynn," he said in a strangled voice, "so, uh, I guess Jimmy and, uh, Sara, they'd be stayin here at the hotel tonight, like you?"

For a moment Bill and Hannah registered mild amazement at the spectacle of the talking Crabbe. Then Bill chuckled softly, saying: "Well, we did offer to put them up—"

"But," finished Hannah, "Jimmy wanted to sleep with Sara. I mean"—she blushed furiously—"in the house he bought her." She brayed her horse laugh.

Crabbe asked where Sara's house was. Intoxicated by the occasion (and by each other), Bill and Hannah were serenely unsuspicious of the normally tongue-tied boy, and told him.

The band started playing "Alexander's Ragtime Band." Sam's driving rhythms had both the fiddler and the banjo player stomping their feet as they played along, and the women from Crapper Jack's spontaneously formed a line and began doing their famous cakewalk, shaking their legs and showing their colorful stockings. The crowd cheered. Hannah blushed again and covered her eyes—then peeked through her fingers, laughing, as Bill rubbed her back.

Zachary Crabbe seemed to be edging his way around the perimeter of the room, and Elly continued to tail him. She was wondering if he was about to confirm her worst fears by leaving, when she realized people were calling her name. She sighed, realizing it had been inevitable, and quickly made her way to the stage. Barely glancing at Sam, she leapt on the bench, murmured "'Jeannie with the Light Brown

Hair' in F" to the other two musicians, and plunged into a *rubato* fantasia on the song. And—in spite of her distracted state—at once lost herself in the music.

Because, of course, she was playing for Jimmy.

She played of his lost sister, Liddie—"Liddie with the light brown hair." She played of all their years together, their travels and adventures. Picnic Pete was in the song, and Professor Carp as well...

The room had gone silent, even the banjo player and fiddler raptly listening.

She soared to the high note of the last phrase, lingered—then struck up a slow, lilting rhythm, glancing at the fiddler. He nodded and began to play the melody, while the banjo player strummed a soft, repeating figure. People in the crowd were swaying their hips to the music; a few began to dance. They went twice through the tune, Elly improvising a sweeping, rhapsodic countermelody until, on the final phrase, she went back into *rubato* and the other musicians dropped out.

The last chord seemed to ring forever and ever...

There was a breathless silence, then the room burst into applause. Sam beamed at her. Jimmy was staring at her with a twisted smile, his eye glistening. She turned her head and searched for Crabbe.

He was gone.

She leapt off the stage, pushed her way through the crowd, paying not the slightest attention to the astonished looks. Out the door, down a hallway to the lobby of the hotel—

Still no sign of him.

Through the lobby, garnering more looks, and out onto the main street. The evening air was cool (but unseasonably warm for Cripple Creek) and groups of people were strolling around, enjoying it.

Far down the street a gangly youth was hurrying quickly away.

She hiked up her bridesmaid gown and ran. The sky was clear, with a moon two days short of full adding its radiance to the gas-lit street, and people stared at her. When she was a block away, she slowed to match his pace. For several more blocks he hurried on with what looked like urgent purpose. Toward the edge of town the street lights ended, and she was able to get even closer. And knew, with a terrible certainty, that she'd been right: it was Tutt's house he was headed for.

Her pale silk gown was terribly conspicuous in the moonlight, and she tried to keep to the shadows as she followed him up the drive. She hid behind some scrub oak and watched him knock on the tall, massive door and—after a short wait—be admitted. Not five minutes later he emerged with something in his hand. He strolled right past her hiding place, a look of satisfaction on his homely features. And she saw that what he held was a roll of bills.

She was debating whether to follow him, return to the hotel, or stay and wait for developments—when she heard a door slam, and the latter course of action decided itself. She edged around the side of the house, still keeping to the shadows, and saw electric lights wink on in the carriage house. She ran quickly toward it and carefully put her face to the window in the double doors. Under the electric lights, the Pierce-Arrow's rich forest green seemed to glow. A figure was moving around, and she realized it was the chauffeur. He had exchanged his uniform for dark clothing and cap. He climbed into the automobile and started the engine. When the powerful machine began to thrum, he climbed back out and disappeared from view, only to return a few seconds later carrying a shotgun.

He threw it onto the front passenger seat and started toward the double doors. Elly jumped to the side and pressed herself against the wall. The doors swung open, and a moment later the huge automobile nosed slowly out, then stopped. She flattened herself against the wall and held her breath. The doors swung shut, and her heart skipped as she stood nakedly revealed. But the chauffeur had already turned around and was climbing back into the vehicle. He threw it in gear and began to motor down the hill—

With Elly standing on the rear bumper and clinging for dear life.

Without her hobo experience, she doubted she could have stayed on the huge automobile as it bumped and swayed its way down the rutted drive. They turned onto the main road. The girl in the flapping bridesmaid gown clinging to the back of the long limousine gathered some truly startled looks from the people strolling along. But they saw her only after the vehicle had passed by, so the driver was unaware.

A few blocks farther they turned onto Sara's street and cruised slowly past the darkened house. At the end of the street the driver made a three-point turn, reversed down the street, then parked under a tree. They were across from the house, but far enough away that Elly doubted they were noticeable in the shadows.

The engine was shut off. Elly stood on the bumper, hardly daring to breathe. Too late she realized that she should have jumped off earlier, for now the slightest movement might betray her presence. Yet she knew she had to somehow get off and make her way back to the hotel.

She was still working up her courage when the carriage Bill had rented turned into the street and clopped its way to Sara's house. She watched as the driver dismounted and helped Jimmy extricate Jonah's wheelchair from the back. Jimmy lifted Jonah into his chair and tipped the driver, who drove off. The three of them entered the house, and a moment later a light came on inside.

She racked her brains for what she could possibly do if the chauffeur went after them right away. But he had lit a cigarette and seemed content to just sit for a while. She decided to try and make her way to the house without his noticing. Her heart beating wildly, she carefully lowered one foot from the bumper to the ground and — with agonizing slowness — transferred her weight from one leg to the other. Finally she stepped completely off, certain she must have jarred the vehicle. But she remained undetected, and was reminded of how battleship-heavy the huge automobile was.

Moving quietly, she went farther up the street — away from Sara's house and the driver's line of vision — then darted along the side of a house into its back yard. Feeling as conspicuous as someone dressed as a spook in a sheet, she hiked up her ridiculous gown and began working her way through a string of back yards toward Sara's house, fighting her way through bushes and climbing over fences—and praying she wouldn't encounter any dogs.

Her gown was muddy and torn by the time she reached Sara's back yard. Lights from the parlor were dimly visible through the kitchen window. The back door was unlatched and she let herself in. She heard sobbing, Sara's voice saying, "…because I just *know* it! I *know* it was him!" She made her way to the parlor and found them both on the sofa, Sara's face buried in Jimmy's shoulder. Both of them looked up at her in mute astonishment.

"You need to leave," said Elly.

"What?" said Sara in a tiny, confused voice.

"Elly," said Jimmy, "Sara jus—well, she jus told me Tutt's driver, well she thinks he's the one shot her daddy."

"I *know* he is!" wailed Sara.

Elly nodded—it all made sense. "He's parked down the street. Zachary Crabbe just told Tutt about Sara—"

"Crabbe!" cried Jimmy. "Why that low-down— Say! I 'member him listenin in on me and Pinky once—"

"And I'm sure," said Elly, cutting him off, "I'm sure the driver has orders to kill her."

Sara moaned. Jimmy set his jaw and pulled the derringer from his coat pocket.

Elly looked at him hard. "He has a shotgun," she said.

They heard a noise and looked up to find Jonah wheeling himself down the hall in his nightshirt. Jimmy looked at him, then back at Elly. Finally he sighed and put away his gun.

"You need to leave right now," said Elly. "Out the back. Leave the light on."

"Sary, what's happenin?" said Jonah. "What's wrong?"

"Ain't nothin wrong, Jonah," said Jimmy brightly. "Yer wanner go fer a walk?"

Jonah stared at him with big eyes.

"Jonah," said Sara.

He looked at her questioningly, saw something in her eye, then said, "All right."

Jimmy rose, lifted Jonah from his chair and onto his back, and the three of them followed Elly out the back door.

"You got to be *quiet!*" Sara hissed in Jonah's ear, and he nodded. Sara hadn't changed yet, and she and Elly both had to hike up their gowns as they made their way through three more backyards toward the main street. Just before they reached it, a dog began feverishly barking, and they broke into a run.

They made it the few blocks to Hannah's house, and Elly pointed to her Roadster.

"We need to leave town."

"Huh?" said Sara, still catching her breath. "But can't we just—"

The desperate situation rendered Elly suddenly articulate, and she interrupted Sara:

"The people who want you killed are just too powerful. Not just Tutt, but the other mine owners are probably involved. What you know could send them all to prison."

"Somebody wants to kill Sary?" cried Jonah, stricken.

"Hey now, pardner," said Jimmy, "don't you worry. They might have their sights set on her, but we're gonna put one over on em. Cause we's leavin town, just like Elly says."

She flashed him a grateful look, then ran into the house. It was dark and empty, everyone still at the reception. She went straight to her room and, without even pausing to light her lamp, tore off her ruined gown and donned overalls, boots, and a fleece-lined jacket. She threw a few things—including her velvet gown, tuning wrench, and Mr. Hoppy—into her valise. Finally she pulled the blankets from her bed and raced back outside.

The others were already in the Roadster. She handed her valise to Jimmy, passed the blankets to Sara and Jonah in the back seat, and cranked the engine. The plucky vehicle started right up. She jumped in, donned cap and goggles and, with the Roadster's lamps still unlit, pulled out onto the main street.

To get to Colorado Springs they had to follow the main road out of town, which meant passing the street where Sara's house was. They were half a block away when two circles of light began pooling at the mouth of the street. Jimmy yelled for Sara and Jonah to get down, there was confusion as he twisted in his seat and tried to cover them with the blankets, they drove past the street—

And past the twin headlamps of the Pierce-Arrow.

Elly glanced in the mirror mounted above the windshield, and watched as the limousine turned onto the street behind them. She thought there was still a chance they hadn't been recognized, and throttled up. They gathered speed, passed the driveway to Tutt's house, then swerved to avoid a slow-moving buggy. Again she glanced in the mirror, hoping the Pierce-Arrow would turn up the drive.

It came implacably on, its speed increasing.

Jimmy let out a curse, and yelled at Sara and Jonah to keep their heads down. Elly throttled all the way up. A moment later they were going full tilt, but she could tell the powerful limousine was still gaining. On the outskirts of town she tore past another buggy—on its way, perhaps, to Victor from the wedding reception—and the horse reared in alarm. A minute later she watched in her mirror as the Pierce-Arrow slowed down to get past the nervous animal, and noted how slowly the big heavy automobile accelerated afterward.

But she knew it would soon catch up.

The two vehicles raced for the rim of the valley, the limousine steadily gaining on them, and when they reached the top of the hill it was only fifty yards behind them. She lit her lamps and started down the switchback, bouncing over the rutted road on the straight parts and tearing around the hairpin curves so fast the inside wheels briefly left the ground. In the back seat she could hear Jonah whimpering. The much heavier Pierce-Arrow was forced to slow down much more on the curves, then took longer to accelerate, and they gained on it.

At the bottom of the hill they came to the creek. Far above them the tops of the trees were illuminated by the headlamps of the approaching limousine. She hesitated only an instant—then plunged in. Sara gave a startled cry and Jimmy looked at Elly. "Don't worry," she said. She lifted her legs, and he copied her. The black water swirled around them. A sudden glare of light splashed the water with gold and for the first time they heard the deep, leonine purr of the monstrous vehicle's huge six-cylinder engine. Once again Jonah whimpered. They climbed up the opposite bank just as they heard the Pierce-Arrow come to a stop, then plunge into the water.

Again the Roadster's ability to take tight curves won them time as they see-sawed up the side of the mountain. At the top the moon suddenly appeared above the treetops and they tore down the road that hugged the canyon wall at an insane rate. Jimmy looked past Elly to the the other side of the moonlit canyon a half-mile away. There was nothing between their car and the canyon walls but black void. Jimmy felt sick, and turned his attention to the road. But it was almost worse—it seemed at any second they might fly off the edge of the ruined track—and he glanced at Elly. She was driving with the same furious intensity with which she played the piano. He looked behind them.

A pair of headlamps winked into view.

He watched until he was sure the other vehicle was gaining on them. He saw Elly register the same thing in her mirror. They swerved around a curve—and almost plowed into where an avalanche of dirt and stones blocked the road. There seemed to be tracks leadng around the edge. Elly threw the Roadster into low gear and began to follow them. Their outside wheels skirted so close to the edge that Jimmy had to look away to fight his terror.

The opposite side of the canyon was lit up with something much brighter than moonlight. Sara peered over the back seat and gave an inarticulate cry. They heard the deep rumble of the Pierce-Arrow's engine as it rounded the curve and came to a stop on the other side of the avalanche. Behind the glare of the limousine's headlamps, Jimmy could make out the driver's silhouette as he rose from his seat. Jimmy yelled, "GET DOWN!" just before a terrible blast ripped through the air. Sara and Jonah screamed. They cleared the obstacle and began to accelerate. Another blast—the Roadster banged as if struck by a baseball bat. More screams as the gunshots ricocheted around the canyon like someone cracking a bullwhip.

Elly heard Jimmy determine that no one was hurt, and throttled up. The ruined road seemed set on shaking the Roadster apart, but they made it to the canyon floor in one piece and tore at top speed down the gravel track. Stones banged against their undercarriage like gunshots. From high above them the moon shone serenely down on their desperate flight with a calmness that seemed ironic. In its ghostly light the gigantic boulders littering the plain looked more like ruined castles than ever, and Elly was just daring to hope that the larger automobile had been unable to clear a way through the avalanche when a pair of headlamps appeared in her mirror like the eyes of some malevolent beast.

Jimmy let out a groan.

On the straight, level road Elly knew they would soon be overtaken by the powerful limousine, and she cursed herself for not dousing her lights earlier and finding some place in the shadow of a boulder to hide. At the same moment, she recognized the stand of aspen marking where she and Lucas had taken the side road up to the abandoned mine. Her mind flashed on the memory of how steep the hill had been, and gave her a sudden idea.

She pulled to a stop just past the road, doused her lights, threw the Roadster into reverse, and began backing up the hill.

She still had a vague hope their pursuer wouldn't notice the ruse and instead go flying past them. But he must have noted exactly where her lights winked out, because he began to slow down, and stopped below them. She could almost feel the huge limousine shifting into its lowest gear, and a moment later it started up after them.

Her great hope had been that the heavy vehicle would not be able to make it up the steep grade—but it came implacably on. Her head was twisted around as she negotiated the road's twists and turns by moonlight, and she saw the gaping hole of the mine's entrance above them. The wild thought came to her that they might be able to hide in the mine. But she and Lucas had found the entrance cluttered with debris, and if the way was blocked, they would be easy targets.

They reached the end of the road, and with despair she realized she had led them into a trap. They could hear the Pierce-Arrow's powerful engine laboring as it climbed doggedly toward them. It rounded the last bend, the glare of its headlamps blinding her—

She made a sudden mad decision.

"Everybody stay down!" she ordered.

She threw the vehicle in high gear—and started back down.

The Roadster was facing forward, and she quickly built up speed until they were bucking over the rutted track. The limousine lurched to a stop, as though the vehicle itself had been given pause by the sight of the Roadster hurtling toward it. She throttled up the engine to top speed, careening down the hill at an insane rate, aimed straight at the Pierce-Arrow. And prayed that, forced to choose between raking them with the shotgun or pulling over to let them pass on the narrow track, the driver would opt for self-preservation…

The glare of headlamps filled her vision, she imagined the flaming wreck about to end their lives—then at the last moment the limousine lunged forward to one side of the road. They tore by so close that the air between the two vehicles buffeted their side and set them wildly rocking. A few seconds later another shotgun blast shattered the air, and the Roadster was battered by a deafening hail of buckshot from behind. Once more Sara yelled, over the sounds of Jonah's sobs, that they were unhurt.

At the bottom of the hill they turned onto the last leg of the road to Colorado Springs, a part of the road Elly and Lucas had never reached. The Pierce-Arrow must have backed slowly down the hill, for they gained at least a mile before its headlamps reappeared in her mirror. But it quickly narrowed the distance on the straight road, and

Elly could only hope there might be another series of hairpin curves so they could again pull ahead.

But the valley ended in a straight road cut into the side of mountain. The lights of Colorado Springs were arrayed below them like a mirror image of the starlit sky. The road descended at a frightening rate, but she drove furiously on, hunched forward, scanning the ruined road and swerving to avoid rocks and ruts, knowing a blowout would be the end of them. In a corner of her mind she thought how lucky they were that the shotgun hadn't punctured their tires or made the gas can in back explode. The thought reminded her of something Harold Baxter had read aloud from the paper about a primitive sort of bomb that the Russian anarchists were now employing—and gave her a sudden, mad inspiration.

She glanced in the mirror. The Pierce-Arrow was perhaps a hundred yards behind them.

"Get the gas can from the back!" she yelled. Jimmy flashed her a look of dazed incomprehension, then scrambled over the back seat where Sara and Jonah lay clutching each other, and came back with the two gallon can.

"Does it have any holes?"

Jimmy checked. "No."

"Find a rag, a piece of cloth, anything!" she commanded.

Jimmy looked wildly around, then pulled out his knife. Bouncing crazily in his seat, he managed to cut a strip from his shirt tail.

"Loosen the cap and dangle it inside," yelled Elly. "Then screw the cap back on so it's half in and half out. Tight—or it will explode when you light it."

Jimmy gaped at her—then followed her instructions. The huge limousine was closing the distance fast, perhaps forty yards behind them now. She guessed the chauffeur would wait until he was so close he couldn't miss, shoot for their tires—and send them hurtling over the edge.

"Wait until he's really close," she yelled, fighting the road. "Don't let him see you until the last minute—then light it and throw it on the road in front of him."

In truth, she knew, it should have been a bottle. What if the can didn't break open? But it was full, the weight should split the seams of the cheap metal. Even so, the limousine would probably just drive unscathed through the flames...

Jimmy twisted the cap on tight and climbed in back with Sara and Jonah, yelling at them to stay down. He crouched low behind the folded canvas top, pulled out his gold lighter, and peered over the edge. The Pierce-Arrow was thirty yards away, careening down the old wagon trail, hurtling toward them... Twenty yards, the huge automobile roaring like a beast about to pounce on them... Ten yards away, and the driver rose shakily to his feet, one hand on the wheel, balanced the shotgun on the windshield—

Jimmy lit the rag, took aim, and hurled the gas can. It flew in a steep arc, over the windshield and into the limousine—*WHUMP!* A flash of light so bright it blinded him for a moment. When he blinked again the cab was awash in flame, the Pierce-Arrow a huge lamp and its driver a human wick, waving flaming arms and screaming—

A scrabbling sound as the huge flaming vehicle sailed over the edge, both the roar of its engine and the screams of its flaming occupant quickly fading away. A discreet explosive *thump,* a small burst of light in the trees far below them, then a minute later everything was swallowed by the night.

They drove on.

THE END OF VOLUME TWO

CONTINUED IN VOLUME THREE:
ELLY ROBIN ON THE ROAD

Afterword and Historical Notes

The clash between the Western Federation of Miners and government troops in Cripple Creek was part of a larger landscape, in the early decades of the twentieth century, of confrontation between organized labor and authority—an authority often cynically aligned with or manipulated by the moneyed class. The details of this violent history, as narrated by Emma Langdon, are all accurate, including the feisty linotype operator's own story. Though Harry Orchard's true role—inept terrorist, or paid agitator?—continues to be argued by historians.

A man suspected of being a witness to the Independence Depot explosion was indeed roused in the middle of the night by masked gunmen and, like Sara's father, murdered in front of his family.

Of the many books that helped me, two stand out. Anne Ellis's modestly titled *The Life of an Ordinary Woman* is a gem of an account of growing up in Colorado mining towns written by a woman who was actually rather extraordinary; I have tried to bring her to life in the character of Hannah. And *Cripple Creek Days*, by Mabel Barbee Lee, provided me with a trove of lore specific to that colorful town, including her eye-witness description of the fabulous cave full of gold crystals discovered in the Cresson mine. I have moved the date back from 1913 to 1912 for the purposes of my story, and the real owner of the Cresson, a man named Dick Roelofs, was already happily married when he finally struck it rich. But I have given Bill Wynn the same attributes of patience, a degree in geology, and a systematic approach to mining. Finally, I hope I may be forgiven one other slight stretching of the truth: though there was indeed a real Crapper Jack's Saloon and Dance Hall, it burned down in the great fire that swept Cripple Creek in 1896. But I found the name just too good to resist.

It should be noted that in 1912 the dollar had roughly twenty times its present value. Thus Elly's $20,000 windfall would have been worth about $400,000 today.

Musical genius is often correlated with mechanical aptitude; the great early-twentieth-century virtuoso Josef Hofmann (himself a child prodigy) reportedly preferred tinkering in his machine shop to playing the piano, and was responsible for several patents. In this book Elly's own mechanical affinities, hinted at in the first book, are finally developed.

The Model T Ford was indeed a marvel of advanced engineering, and rather infamous for having more power in reverse than first gear; you were better off going up a steep hill backwards. The 1911 models actually were available in an array of colors like the blue of Elly's roadster; it was only later that Henry Ford limited the selection to "any color you want, so long as it's black."

In a time when a child can hardly grow up without accidentally stumbling on Internet pornography, it may seem preposterous that twelve-year-old Elly—despite years of exposure to hobo camps and saloons—could still be ignorant of the actual mechanics of sex. But in 1912, such things were still utterly unmentionable (a holdover from the Victorian era), contributing to a general ignorance of all things sexual that seems, to our own jaded era, almost unbelievable.

The Lonely Villa, the early silent picture Elly and her friends see in Colorado Springs, was a 1909 film directed by D. W. Griffith, and one of the earliest examples of the use of cross-cutting to ramp up the excitement of a story. It was a technique that would add to the power of his controversial masterpiece of 1915, *The Birth of a Nation*.

In all the books, I have tried to be scrupulously accurate when introducing music of the period, and "Alexander's Ragtime Band" was indeed a monster hit of 1911. There were also songs that were regional hits, to which I can attest, for I once had the experience, in the early 1980's, of playing in several Colorado nursing homes. And found "When It's Springtime in the Rockies" could bring tears to the eyes of people who might have been courting that very year.

I hope you enjoyed the second volume of Elly's adventures. As always, I welcome any comments from my readers, and promise to respond to them.

Sincerely,
P.D. Quaver
contact at: pdquaver.com

Suggested Listening

In this volume of our story, Elly receives some essential lessons in the art of playing ragtime.

There is still some disagreement regarding what tempo ragtime should be played, stemming from Scott Joplin's admonitions, printed on many of his rags, that ragtime should "never be played fast." One could infer from this, though, that many of his contemporaries *were* playing this music at a tempo he considered too fast! It should also be noted there were regional differences; the ragtime of New Orleans (exemplified by the music of Jelly Roll Morton) and Joplin's native Missouri was slower, while East Coast ragtime tended to be faster and snappier, and led to the early virtuosic jazz style known as "stride piano." Whatever the tempo, it's important to remember that ragtime was, first and foremost, dance music—specifically for the contemporary dance craze the "cakewalk"—and needs to be full of life. An example of how *not* to play ragtime can be found the Nonesuch recording of Joplin Rags by Joshua Rifkin, part of the "ragtime revival" of the seventies; it is impossible to imagine dancing to these staid renditions.

All this said, here are a few recordings you might enjoy:

Scott Joplin: "Gladiolus Rag," played by Max Morath

Max Morath, who performed one-man shows on Broadway specializing in turn-of-the-century music, was one of the most stylish players of ragtime. His playing combined a wonderful rhythmic swing with a freedom from the printed score in keeping with how ragtime was actually played; I can't recommend his recordings highly enough.

James Scott: "Frog Legs Rag"

If you are familiar only with Joplin, you should check out some of the pyrotechnic rags of James Scott. This snappy recording is by Ragtime Dorian Henry.

Themola London Pianola: "Alexander's Ragtime Band" (1928)

A stylish, strutting rendition of Irving Berlin's monster hit from 1911.

The Heidelberg Quintette: "Waiting for the Robert E. Lee"

A contemporary recording, from 1912, of another of the era's huge hits.

Ignaz Friedman: Chopin "Minute Waltz" (1924)

The popular misunderstanding (shared by the characters in this book) that Chopin's waltz in D-flat was meant to be played in a minute, stems from an English publisher who retitled it the "Minute" (as in my-NOOT) waltz. This sprightly performance, by one of the great virtuosos of the early twentieth century, still clocks in at 1:34. Incidentally, check out Friedman's amazing performance of the final run in double thirds!

Acknowledgments

Many friends read the first drafts of "the Elly books," as I often call them, and offered countless valuable suggestions. I would like to especially thank Doc D., Al H., Fred K., "Swede," Mike G., Michael B., and Kevin U.

Elly's most devoted (if not entirely unbiased) fan was my mother, whose delight in the first four volumes of my tale kept me going. Though she passed away when the work was yet unfinished (as it still is as I write this!), she remains my "ideal reader."

Finally, five people deserve special mention: Sandy K., for her unshakeable faith in both myself and my project; Steve C., ace researcher; Kathy O., who graciously agreed to offer her skills as editor; and my two hyper-literate and discerning brothers. Without the love and support of this formidable quintet, Elly would never have been brought to life; I can never thank them enough.

Sincerely, P.D. Quaver

About the Author

P.D. Quaver is a retired musician. In a long life as a professional pianist, he has played everything from Bach and Beethoven to jazz, ragtime and blues, including most everything the fictional Elly Robin performs in his books. In addition to "The Ordeals of Elly Robin" series, he is the author of the young adult thriller *Unplugged*. He divides his time between Colorado and Washington State.

Made in the USA
Monee, IL
16 May 2022

96522141R00115